SHADOWS

AN EMP SURVIVAL THRILLER

AMERICAN MIDNIGHT
BOOK 1

DAVID KAZZIE

ISBN-13: 978-1733134194

ISBN-10: 1733134190

❀ Created with Vellum

First, as Always, For My Kids
May You Someday Think of Me as a Real Writer

And to the healthcare workers, first responders, grocery store clerks, truck drivers, farmers, food industry workers, and all other essential workers carrying us through the coronavirus pandemic

ALSO BY DAVID KAZZIE

THE JACKPOT (2011)

THE IMMUNE (2015)

THE LIVING (2017)

ANOMALY (2018)

THE NOTHING MEN (2019)

1

More than anything, Lucy Goodwin wanted to get home.

They had been on the train for four hours already, today's journey from Philadelphia to Washington, D.C., aboard the crowded southbound Acela taking more than twice as long as it should have. The train had been scheduled to leave three minutes past seven, but it was closer to eight before they got underway, and Lucy was already two terrible cups of coffee into this terrible day. And once underway, they could never get up to a good cruising speed. Somewhere in northern Maryland, the conductor had fired up the intercom to inform them that a pickup truck had broken down on the tracks and that cost them another forty minutes.

Ordinarily, Lucy loved traveling by train, the methodical clackety-clack of the train cars rolling along the steel tracks a welcome salve to the stress of her life. It was soothing, much more so than air travel. For medium-range travel, you couldn't beat the train. But it had been a long three days at the annual nursing conference in Philadelphia; she had been out of sorts from the moment she set foot in the convention hall, waiting in line for her name badge and her bag of useless swag. What a waste those bags were. Coupons and magazines and stress balls and drink koozies and all manner of junk that more often than not ended up in a landfill. As if the planet didn't have enough junk to deal with.

The National Nursing Council's annual conference was typically one of the high points of Lucy's year. Although she loved being a nurse, it was nice to get a break from the rigor of her twelve-hour shifts, and the continuing education seminars were always instructive. Plus, she got to catch up with nursing school friends who'd scattered across the country over the years. But by the middle of the first day, she was done with it. She began counting down the days, then the hours, and then the minutes until it was over.

Instead of dining with her fellow nurses, she took her meals alone, not in the mood to spend a week with five hundred other nurses, drinking, gossiping, complaining. During the sessions, she sat in the back row, doodling in the small notebook that had been inside her tote bag. She missed her patients, she missed the E.R., she missed her dog. She even missed Jack, her pain-in-the-ass brother.

But it was over.

She sighed.

It was finally over.

It was Friday, and they would be home by dinnertime. Soon, she would be on her couch in her pajama pants and sweatshirt, eating General Tso's chicken from Peking and binge-watching something mind-blowingly idiotic. Maybe a good reality show about housewives with too much money and not enough sense. She would sleep in, as she wasn't due back at the hospital for her next shift until Sunday morning.

Next to her sat Manuel Diaz, her fellow E.R. nurse at the Henrico Doctors' Hospital, a suburban hospital just west of Richmond, Virginia. He was a nice enough fellow who'd come to nursing later in life. He was a decent nurse but a bit chauvinistic. Rarely showed deference to more experienced female nurses, seemed to think he knew better than them. Patients loved him though, which made him a formidable coworker.

He'd been asleep since they pulled out of the 30th Street Station in Philly. She'd gone to bed early the night before, but he'd stayed up partying with a contingent of nurses from Tampa. When they'd met at the continental breakfast at five-thirty that morning, he had still reeked of cheap liquor and cigarette smoke. He obviously hadn't slept. Whatever. As long as he didn't puke on her.

The train was moving along at a good clip, finally, after an eternity at a snail's pace. Outside, the landscape flew by in a flash. They were south of Baltimore now, hopefully no less than thirty minutes from Union Station. There, they would switch engines for the last two hours to Richmond, where Lucy had lived for the last fifteen years.

She turned her attention back to the e-book reader on her lap; her book club was reading a novel about a teenage boy who loses his mother in a terrorist bombing of a museum and the priceless piece of art that he steals in the ensuing chaos. It was beautifully written, but the story just had not held Lucy's interest. She flipped through a couple more pages before her attention waned once more. She checked her reading progress. Thirty-four percent into the eight-hundred-page novel. The book club was scheduled to meet the following night. Yeah, well, she didn't think the other women in the club would read it either. And if they did, she could certainly fake her way through it. Besides, a healthy chunk of any good book club involved drinking wine and gossiping about the women who hadn't shown up that night.

"Where are we?" Manny asked, startling her.

The big man stretched and let out a long breath.

Yup, still whiskey-tinged, thought Lucy.

"Just south of Baltimore," Lucy said.

"Cool," he said.

Cool. Everything was cool to Manny. Giving report on a shift change, cool. Headed out for a smoke break, cool. Asteroid headed toward earth, cool.

"That was a good conference," he said.

"I guess."

"You didn't enjoy it?"

"It was fine," she said, anxious to shut off this line of

conversation. She closed her eyes and pictured herself on the couch with her carton of Chinese food.

"You should have come out with us," he said, yawning.

"I was tired," she said.

He waved a dismissive hand at her.

"You always say that," Manny said. "You hardly ever go out with us. You're such a homebody."

This was true. If she wasn't at work, she preferred to be at home. Out in the country with her dog and the animals and the farm and the trees. In her downtime, she liked to read and drink tea like an old lady. Sometimes, she felt like an old woman. She'd certainly suffered enough for one lifetime. She hoped that she wouldn't have to endure any more heartache.

Either way, Lucy's partying days were long behind her. She was thirty-nine years old and she didn't bounce back from a twelve-hour shift like she used to. She envied the exuberance of her younger coworkers, many of whom she had by a decade or more. But that was how it went. You had your time in the sun, and then you moved out of its glare. Or more accurately, you were pushed out of its glare.

"I'm old and tired."

A dismissive wave.

"I'm older than you!" he replied. "Seriously, Luce, it's no good for you to just shut yourself off like that all the time. Anyway. We missed you. Had the best cheesesteak at four this morning!"

And that was Manny. Guy was even older than Lucy was. But he'd only been a nurse for three years, having spent years working as a paralegal for a real estate firm. Then he decided that nursing was his true calling and went through the bachelor's degree program that the hospital offered. He was relatively new to the profession, but time did not care. Nursing was a tough job in your twenties, and he hadn't gotten his license until he was almost forty. His downfall was coming sooner than he expected. Especially if he was up eating cheesesteaks at four in the morning.

"'Best cheesesteak in Philly', they said."

"I'm sure they all say that."

"Man, it was good."

"I'm sure your body will appreciate that," she replied.

"My body is a temple," he said. Then he leaned back and closed his eyes again.

She shook her head. Nurses and doctors were notoriously bad at taking care of themselves. She didn't know if it was a middle finger to Death, the battle those in her profession were constantly fighting and losing, or the stress of the job itself, dealing with people who did not follow their advice or who ended up in her emergency room for the dumbest, most preventable reasons possible. Kids overdosing on prescription medication they had found in their parents' closets. Young adults who hadn't buckled their seatbelts rocketing through windshields. Gunshot victims were the hardest, especially the young victims. Toddlers who'd found the semi-automatic pistol their careless fathers almost certainly would have never used in self-defense and blown their faces off. She hated guns; she wasn't sure if that it was despite the fact that she'd spent four years in the Army as a medic or because of it.

Stop, she thought.

You did what you could. You fixed the ones you could fix and you sent them on their way. And maybe they would learn their lesson and see that they'd gotten lucky this time, and change their ways and live a bit more carefully or get into rehab or always wear their seatbelt or pay a bit more attention to their kids and a bit less attention to their smartphones.

She set her attention back on her book, but once again, her focus faded after just a few sentences. Maybe it was the delivery system. Maybe she just wasn't one for e-books, no matter how close they came to duplicating actual print with their electronic ink. Maybe if she had a print version of the novel, she would be farther along. Maybe she would even be enjoying it. She loved books; her house was swamped with them. She filled her bookcases as fast as her brother could build them for her.

She turned her gaze back out the window; the landscape rushing by took on a distinctly metropolitan feel as they drew closer to Washington. They were crossing the Anacostia River; Route 50 ran alongside the river, thick with lunch hour traffic. Waves of heat shimmered in the distance. It was another hellaciously hot day.

One more chapter.

She would finish one more chapter before they got to the station. Perhaps she'd bang out another chapter or two at home tonight, getting her closer to the end of a book that wasn't just a book but *award-winning literature.*

She glanced back down at the e-reader; the screen was blank. She hadn't remembered turning it off, but the thing glitched from time to time. Another benefit of print books. You cracked one of those open and the words would be there every time. No battery to worry about. So she often forgot to charge up her electronic reader. To be fair, the device did have a long battery life, and so it was easy to forget that it did, in fact, have a battery. She slid the device back into her backpack. The author's scintillating prose would just have to wait.

Next to her, Manny snored.

Boredom rippled through her. They were in that phase of the trip where you were almost there, so close, but not quite, which made that last bit stretch on interminably. Like that old math trick–if you kept halving the distance you had left to go, you would never get home. Around her, the other passengers appeared to become restless as well. Muted whispers became loud whispers. In fact, she had to admit, they really weren't whispers at all.

The first hint of trouble was the uniformed train attendant virtually sprinting down the aisle toward the locomotive, which was six or seven cars ahead of theirs. He was a tall, thin man; he'd been quite jovial that morning, telling jokes, laughing as he'd scanned the passengers' tickets.

He didn't look jovial anymore.

As he bolted down the aisle, he did not make eye contact with anyone, his gaze focused on the pass-through to the next train car. Something about the look on his face had unnerved Lucy, sending a chill rippling through her. She wondered if a passenger was having a medical emergency. She rose out of her seat and looked around the train car. A number of animated discussions were underway.

In the row in front of Manny, catty corner from Lucy, was a young girl, maybe twelve years old, her nose in a book. A print book! Ha! A kid with more sense than Lucy. Next to her was an elderly black woman. They had boarded the train together; perhaps she was the girl's grandmother.

"Excuse me," a voice said, startling Lucy from her daydreaming surveillance of her train car. A man's face appeared above the seatback in front of her. He was handsome in a traditional sort of way. He wore a suit and had nice hair. A pair of black eyeglasses framed his face just so.

"Sorry to bother you," he said, holding up his phone. "My phone just died, and my charger doesn't seem to be working. Do you have one I can borrow?"

"Uh, yeah, let me see," replied Lucy, digging into her bag. Her charger was connected to her phone; she detached it and handed it to the man.

"Thanks," he said. "Just need to get enough juice to call my wife."

Her gut twisted at that. Not because she had her eye on this man; it was more his life that she was eyeing. And not his actual life. The perfect version of his life—the one that he and his wife posted on social media. Maybe a life that she had dreamed up of whole cloth. The one that filtered out the tedium and boredom of everyday life. For all she knew, this man and his wife detested each other. But it was a life she had been deprived. It was a life she would never have. It was a life permanently scarred with tragedy, a gouge across her soul that would never heal.

He disappeared back into his seat. She lifted her phone to check her messages, which, to her surprise, was dark itself. Now that was weird. It was fully charged when she left the hotel this morning, and she had used it sparingly since boarding the train. She definitely had not turned it off.

Before she had time to process this newest development, a commotion at the front of the train car caught her attention. Another conductor, this one a petite Asian woman, had come into her train car, her arms extended, patting at the air with her hands, as if to tell everyone to quiet down.

"Heads down!" she screeched. "Heads down!"

A bolt of terror rocketed through Lucy as the train car erupted into panic.

As the woman passed her row, Lucy reached out and grabbed her by the arm.

"What's happening?" Lucy asked.

The conductor reared back, trying to break free of the grip, but Lucy would not let go. She was at least eight inches taller than the conductor and outweighed her by fifty pounds.

"Let me go!"

"Just tell me what's happening!" she barked.

The woman relaxed her gyrations and looked Lucy dead in the eye. Beside her, Manuel stirred awake, his eyes wide with confusion.

"The engineer can't stop the train," she said grimly. "Nothing's working. We're going to crash."

Lucy let go of the woman as her words sank in. She disappeared into the next car, shouting her morbid warning.

"The hell did she just say?" Manuel said.

Lucy glanced out the window as the city rushed by in a flash. They were going at least seventy miles per hour.

"My God," she whispered.

Lucy's military training kicked in. Just like that, she was back in Afghanistan, pinned down under Taliban fire, struggling to save a soldier who'd been gut shot. She became hyper-aware of the speed they were traveling, of the train's mammoth size, of the catastrophe that would ensue if it crashed. Of course, this couldn't have happened an hour ago, when they were puttering along at fifteen miles per hour. At that speed, the train would have simply coasted to a halt.

But it was not to be.

They were less than ten miles from Union Station, the large train station in the middle of Washington, D.C. If she recalled correctly, the track curved sharply to the left just before reaching the station. And if the engineer couldn't decelerate, they would likely jump the track there; only God knew what fate awaited them once they were loose of the track's loving embrace.

Full-blown panic had gripped the train car in the wake of the conductor's announcement. No one had assumed the crash position (for all the good it would do them during the train's imminent derailment and buckling of its sixteen cars). Several passengers had their faces glued to the windows as the train screamed toward its destiny.

"Why won't this work? Why won't this work?" a voice was repeating.

She peeked over the seatback; it was the man who'd borrowed her charger, his attention focused on the phone in his trembling hand. The screen was still dark, even though it was plugged into the outlet.

He looked up at Lucy.

"Why won't this thing work?"

She shook her head and sat back down.

"Lucy, what the hell is going on?" Manny asked.

"We need cover," she said.

She stood up again.

"Everybody listen up!" she yelled, her voice slicing through the buzz of the panicked discussions.

Silence dropped across the train car like an anvil; two dozen sets of eyes burrowed in on her, making her profoundly uncomfortable.

"We've only got a couple minutes," she said, sweat slicking her back. "Go through your bags, find anything you can use to cushion the impact. Stick them under your clothes. Cover your heads with the thickest things you've got. Towels, T-shirts, sweaters, things like that. Protect yourself from the waist up as best you can."

The group stood frozen.

"Now, dammit, now!"

The ice of their terror cracked. Within seconds, the passengers were looting their bags, constructing their own makeshift body armor. Lucy did the same, rifling through her duffel bag. Around her head, she wrapped her VCU sweatshirt, the one she had brought to fight the chill in the convention center. Then she stuffed t-shirts and underwear and socks under her shirt to protect her abdomen. When she'd finished putting on her armor, she took a moment to gauge their location. The train was running due south; the danger was still ahead, when the train would hit that terrifying curve.

"Manny," she said, "see if we can get these seat cushions off."

They dug their fingers into the back of their seats and began prying the cushion loose; she didn't know how well-secured they were. As they worked, Manny was breathing rapidly; sweat slicked his face. The poor guy was terrified. She reached over and touched his elbow.

"It's gonna be okay," she said.

Even though she didn't know that.

As the others worked, Manny pried the cushion loose with a mighty tug befitting a man his size.

"Pull up the seat cushions," she yelled, turning her head toward the crowd.

Her heart thumped against her breastbone as she

worked, not thinking about anything but the task at hand. To think too far down the track, figuratively or literally, would mean thinking about the fact that her life might be over in a matter of minutes. She pulled one loose and then another.

The sound of sobbing cutting through the buzz reached her ears. It was the girl who'd been reading the novel. Her eyes were wet and her shoulders were heaving. She was pulling on the cushion, but it was not giving. Her grandmother was small and frail, paralyzed with indecision. Lucy could see it on her face, wrinkled like a relief map. The woman was still in her chair, her hands gripping the armrests so tightly Lucy could see the veins in her paper-thin skin.

"Can I help you all?" Lucy asked.

"Lord, yes," said the woman in a voice scarcely above a whisper. Her gaze was fixed on the window, the landscape screaming by.

She stepped across the aisle to the girl's side. She was petite, thin, and had wire-straight, jet black hair that fell to the middle of her back.

"It'll be okay," she said again, and this time she wanted to believe it. She didn't want the girl to see how frightened she was herself.

"Dig your fingers into the back here," said Lucy, reaching behind the cushion.

The girl mimicked Lucy's actions, and together they pulled it loose.

"Your turn, ma'am," Lucy said, trying to hide the

panic bubbling inside her. They weren't far from the station now.

After the grandmother stood up, bracing herself against the side of the car, Lucy and the girl pulled up her cushion. She lay one cushion down on the ground and handed the second one to the girl.

"Both of you lie down," Lucy said.

The pair complied. It took the old woman a bit longer, but eventually, they were down together. They curled up against one another, tightly holding hands. The girl was slightly larger than her grandmother, and she curled her body around the older woman like a comma.

"Press down on the cushion as hard as you can and hold the second cushion over your head."

"Hold these around your chest and neck, as tightly as you can, okay?"

The girl nodded. Her lower lip was quivering. The grandmother's eyes were shut tight and she was mouthing words, probably in prayer.

"What's your name?" Lucy asked.

"Norah."

"That's a pretty name," Lucy said. "I'm Lucy."

"Are we going to die?" she asked.

Lucy's stomach turned at the question. She didn't want to spook the girl, but she didn't want to sugarcoat things. That never went well. Lucy's life had been nothing but tragedy underneath a saccharine crust that she'd tried to pass off as truth.

"We're gonna protect ourselves as best we can," she said.

"You don't talk like other grownups."

Lucy chuckled, a moment of mirth that drained away as she felt the train hit the curve.

"Remember to hold this tightly over your head," she said. "It's almost time."

"Will you lie down next to me?"

She glanced at the grandmother, who nodded.

"Yes."

She stood up and staggered as the train hit the curve at a dizzying speed. Manny handed her the cushion and they locked eyes. She searched for something to say, but the words would not come. Rarely had she felt so helpless, so utterly at the mercy of forces beyond her control.

"Everyone down!" she screamed as she hit the deck, throwing an arm over the slight bodies of the girl and her grandmother.

The train car groaned as the centrifugal forces now controlling it pushed it beyond its ability to remain wedded to the track. Then it happened. A hiccup in the train's smooth glide followed by a gargantuan roar and the terrific sound of metal crumpling, a deep, bellowing sound. Three heavy thumps, like gunshots dressed in the deepest of bass.

"Lucy!"

She held Norah as tightly as she could, careful to keep the cushion over her head.

Another deafening groan, this one a result of the

sleek, bullet-shaped locomotive jumping the track. Its streamlined design helped the train make good time through the nation's busy northeast corridor, but freed of its moorings, it had become a missile, pulling two dozen warheads along with it. The derailment bloomed exponentially, each collision between train cars worsening the disaster at a geometric rate.

The coupling at the front of Lucy's train car snapped away like a child's toy, leaving it on its own, independent of the disaster engulfing the front half of the train. The force of the decoupling sent their car skidding across the parking lot fronting the station. Then it tipped over, scattering passengers everywhere.

True to her word, Norah held the cushion firm as the derailment flung them across the compartment, the laws of gravity not operating as one would expect. Their bodies slammed into the side wall as the car rolled a second time. Lucy could not tell up from down, but she was still conscious and Norah was screaming, and those were all good things. It meant they were alive.

Screams of pain and howls of anguish filled the passenger car, auditory nightmares that would haunt Lucy for the rest of her days. People were dying all around her; fate would decide who lived and who was seeing their last moments on Earth. And there was nothing she could do but hold on.

The doomed train car was on its side now, sliding through the parking lot and scattering parked cars like bowling pins. Passengers were flung around the cabin like rag dolls; Lucy lost her grip on the girl. Her stomach dropped as she went airborne, freed, briefly, from the bonds of gravity. Then she really was at the hands of fate, as was often the case when death was nearby. In the vortex of sudden disaster, death didn't care. Death was arbitrary and capricious. It would take a healthy teenager and spare a hundred-year-old woman. It felt like she was floating, hell, maybe she was floating, and the world sped up and came to a complete halt all at the same time. If this was the end, perhaps she would see Emma soon.

Then the train car crashed through a bus vestibule, spinning on its horizontal axis until it came to rest at the edge of a café at the corner of the station terminal. The train car was cloudy with dust; the soft moans of the injured and the dying peppered the air. Lucy exhaled softly, afraid to move, afraid to try to move, lest she discover that she was paralyzed. The moment was frozen in time. She breathed in, happy to be taking in breath (*another time, sweet Emma, we will meet another time*).

The girl.

Norah.

"Norah!" she called out.

"Yeah," came a small voice in reply.

"Are you okay?" Lucy whispered.

"I think so."

"Can you wiggle your toes?" Lucy asked.

"Yeah."

This simple act filled Lucy with relief. There would

be bad news ahead, of this she was sure, but it was good to start this nightmare with something positive.

"How about your grandmother?"

"I don't see her."

"What's her name?"

"Yvette."

"Yvette!" Lucy called out. "Yvette!"

She listened carefully. No reply.

"We'll find her in a minute," Lucy said.

"Did you wiggle your toes?" Norah asked.

Lucy had not. She was too afraid to. Paralysis was one of her greatest fears; she could not fathom not being in control of her body. When she had been in Afghanistan, she had feared paralysis far more than death. But she could not lie here like a frightened puppy, a deer frozen in the headlights that was this horrific train crash.

"Do it," Norah said.

"Okay."

She sent the signal down her legs and wiggled her toes. Tears of joy streamed down her face as her body responded to her commands. As she wept, other sounds in the train car began filtering through. Pleas for help and grunts of pain and tears of despair swirled together in a symphony of suffering.

"We need to check on your grandmother," Lucy said. "Stay where you are."

Lucy pushed herself up to her feet and did a quick self-assessment. Small cuts and scrapes striated her arms, but she was otherwise okay. The same, unfortunately, could not be said for Norah's grandmother. Their double seat had broken free during the crash, crushing her against the side of the train's outer shell, which had crumpled inward. Her head was twisted at a grotesque angle; blood pooled underneath her. Lucy crawled toward her and pressed two fingers to the woman's neck. No pulse. She lay her hand on her chest, but she wasn't breathing. There was a blanket bunched up on the floor, and Lucy pulled it over the woman's upper torso and face. She said a small prayer for the woman. If she had suffered, it hadn't been for very long.

"Come with me," she said, using her body to block Norah's view of her grandmother's untimely end.

"Where are we going?"

"See who needs help."

"What about my grandmother?"

Lucy carefully considered her response.

"She's badly hurt," Lucy said. "We need to get her to the hospital."

The train car on its side had a disorienting effect. Lucy was standing on the spider-webbed train car window. Across from her was the man who'd wanted to call his family. He wasn't moving. A twisted piece of metal had pierced his abdomen. Lucy had been a nurse long enough to know that there was nothing she could do for him.

Manny.

She crossed the aisle back to her seat, gingerly step-

ping around a spear of metal that had spiked from the
floor as the car had blown apart.

"Manny!" she called out.

A groan.

"Manny!"

"I'm good!"

Manny was underneath their seat, which had buckled
and flipped over.

"All your parts working?"

"I think so."

"I'm going to lift the edge and you crawl out."

"Got it."

She knelt down on her haunches and tucked her
hands under the edge of the seat. After a mental one-two-
three, she drove her weight into it, lifting it clear of the
ground. It was much heavier than she expected, and she
could only lift it a few inches.

"Now, Manny."

The big man began wiggling his way out of the cavity;
just as her muscles gave out, Manny had moved out far
enough to bear the seat's weight. When he was clear, she
let go, and the seat crashed to the floor with a terrific
thud. He was cut and scratched to hell, but he appeared
to be okay.

"You're bleeding," he said to her, pointing at her forehead. He handed her a crumpled napkin from his pocket.
She pressed it to her head for a few seconds, surprised to
see the amount of blood that soaked it.

"Who needs help?" she called out, turning to face the car.

The replies came in bulk.

Time to do a little triage.

"Listen to me!" she called out. "If you can walk, get clear. I'm a nurse. Are there any doctors or nurses who can help?"

There were no replies.

Manny tapped her on the shoulder and pointed to the front of the train car. Her knees buckled when she saw it. A plume of flame was rippling in the corner like a little campfire. There would be no time for triage. Those who could get out would have to do so right now; many would not get out in time.

"Everyone out, everyone out!" she yelled. "Fire!"

She leaned down and yanked Norah to her feet, nearly pulling the girl's arms out of their sockets. She scanned the compartment for the nearest exit. There was a breach in the train car where it had broken open as it had collided with the car in front of it. The opening, rimmed with jagged metal, look like the mouth of a snarling demon.

Pushing Norah along in front of her, she pulled survivors to their feet and corralled them like cattle. Several could not move, and Lucy had no choice but to leave them.

Triage was a bitch.

A dozen survivors converged at the opening; not bad,

given how cataclysmic the crash had been. One by one they slipped outside as the fire bloomed in size.

"Get away from the train," she said over and over, constantly glancing over her shoulder. The fire was spreading rapidly, filling the inside of the car with sweeping sheets of flame.

Lucy waited until the last person was out, and then she, Norah, and Manny followed out into the smoky afterbirth of the train crash. The heat from the growing blaze warmed her back. Buried deep into her soul were the howls of people trapped in the growing conflagration.

"Run," she said.

The girl's head swiveled back to the doomed train car, but Lucy gently placed a hand on her cheek and kept her looking forward.

"What about my grandmother?"

Lucy locked the girl's hand tight in her own and pulled her along. The survivors from their car sped up, jogging and then sprinting to escape the blaze. When they were a hundred yards clear, the car exploded, spraying the vicinity with scorching hot metal and glass. The blast wave pushed Lucy and Norah to the ground. It was a brutal second cut. Around her, several more people perished instantly, cut down by fiery debris ejected by the explosion.

Lucy climbed back to her feet.

"You okay?" she asked Norah for what seemed like the hundredth time.

The girl stared blankly toward the burning wreckage.

Tears streamed down her dirty face, caked with soot and ash.

"Norah," she said, clapping her hands to capture the girl's attention.

But the girl remained focused on what had become her grandmother's tomb. She gave Norah a few moments to compose herself. To the east, two large fires were burning, belching clouds of black smoke into the sky. Then something new caught her eye.

A large commercial jetliner was approaching from the north, low in the sky. It was descending rapidly, much too rapidly, and she understood grimly that the plane would crash. The wings wobbled from side to side as the pilots struggled to control the aircraft. She willed them to stabilize it; it was unnerving to watch the wings tip violently from one side to another. She could not imagine the horror the passengers would be experiencing as she stood here with her feet safely on the ground.

The plane passed directly overhead, so low she could see the rivets bolted in the airplane chassis. Around her, dozens of people had craned their necks skyward to watch this new disaster unfold on top of their own. Lucy's heart sank as the pilots lost their final battle with physics. The plane flipped upside down and clipped the top of an office building about half a mile to the north, shearing off one wing. The surviving fuselage spun wildly like a top before crashing beyond a ridge of buildings. It exploded on impact, sending a mushroom cloud of black smoke curling into the sky.

As she watched the fire burn, she felt Norah's hand slide into her own.

"What happened?" she asked in a tiny voice.

"I don't know," Lucy replied.

They stood there in a vortex of death and debris and destruction, and for the second time in her life, Lucy felt utterly helpless and alone.

3

The students sat silently, shifting in their seats while their English teacher, Tim Whitaker, waited for an answer. He enjoyed doing this to them, waiting patiently for someone to respond, waiting until the silence became so unbearable that speaking up was preferable to the awkward quiet. They were reading *To Kill a Mockingbird*, discussing whether Atticus Finch, perhaps the most famous hero in American literature, was, in fact, a hero or if he was just a little less shitty than the other white characters populating Harper Lee's novel.

It was eleven-thirty-eight in the morning, third period at Westerberg High School in Arlington, Virginia. Honors English, which, in theory, meant the kids were academically motivated, driven by an invisible engine under the hood. This was Tim's fourteenth year teaching, and he loved it. He loved all of it. Especially the kids. They were terrible and wonderful and impulsive and brilliant, and growing up online connected to one another helped them see that they were not alone, that they were capable of great things because they could see others like them who did great things.

He stole a quick glance at the clock hanging on the wall. Twenty minutes before this class ended and these two dozen students marched off to lunch, their favorite class of the day. He stood at the front of the classroom, his arms folded across his broad chest, the fingers of his right hand tapping his left bicep. The sound was huge in the massive silence of the room.

Students hated being called on, but they hated speaking up even more. Even the ones who liked the subject, the ones who read the book and wanted to discuss it. But speaking up without being called on was anathema to these sixteen and seventeen-year-olds. That was why he took this approach; he wanted them to participate, to find it within themselves to speak up. Speaking up when it was difficult to do so wasn't just important in his Honors English class. It would be important wherever they went in life.

Tim did not remind the students that he would wait as long as it took in this class and the next and even the next for someone to speak up. Because the quality of the classroom discussion was always very high when the students started the discussion, even at the expense of lost classroom time. He prowled the aisles from one side of the classroom to the other, waiting, waiting. Students shifted in their seats. Knuckles cracked, sighs were sighed.

"Come on," someone whispered.

He smiled as he passed by.

"He's not a racist!"

He chuckled softly. The dam had broken. It was Violet Adams, a very bright senior.

"Go on," he said.

Violet was quite striking, a tall redhead. His friends often teased him about being around beautiful high school girls. *How can you stand it,* they would ask. *You must go home and jerk off after school every day.*

The truth was that he was never tempted. Never. When you were with these kids day after day, it became painfully obvious, no matter how well the girls wore the tight jeans and short shorts and shirts that barely covered their midriffs, that they were just that – kids. It was his job to shepherd these kids to the dawn of their adulthood as best as he could. He took it very seriously, even if there were some days he wanted to throw it all right in the trash. The damage he could do to them was incalculable, and he never forgot it.

"He taught Scout that all men were created equal," she continued.

He agreed with her, more or less, but he wanted to explore all sides of the issue. And he didn't think that Lee's Atticus was a saint. All white people were racist to a certain extent. Even if you believed in equal opportunity for all, even if you believed that blacks had been dealt the worst possible hand, that the echoes of slavery reverberated today, more than a hundred and fifty years after its eradication. You still drove through the projects with both hands wrapped tightly on the wheel and your gander up. It was just the way it was. Tim was black, and even he had done it. So he knew damn well that every single white person who had ever lived had profiled a person of a different race.

"Anyone want to argue the other side?"

He didn't teach *Go Set a Watchman*, the sorry so-called sequel that had been published not too many years before. It was obviously an early draft of *Mockingbird*, nothing more than a cash grab by the publisher. In his mind, the book didn't even exist.

"Oh, he's racist," said Melvina, one of the few African-American students in the class.

A flutter of joy. He loved it when this happened, when the kids could debate these things in this forum, debates that would better them as people long after they left the hallowed halls of this institution. He believed that literature was the great leveler, the great teacher. Not only did it show you the world through someone else's eyes, through the eyes of the character, it showed you the world through the eyes of other readers, those who would see a story in an entirely different way.

That was when the lights went out.

"Ohhhhh," the students said in unison.

Tim sighed. Power outages weren't unheard of, but they weren't common either. The classroom was on the east side of the building, and it was a sunny day, so the room stayed bright as they wound their way toward the noon hour. He would have to move quickly before he lost control of the day's session; the discussion had finally borne fruit.

"We're gonna keep going," he said without missing a beat, knowing the kids' knee-jerk reaction would be to reach for their phones. He had a strict no-phones policy in class, and so they remained in their backpacks or pockets for the duration of the class. They weren't even allowed to have them out as they entered the classroom.

"I'm sure it'll be back on in a minute," he said. "The generators will kick on. Melvina, you were saying?"

"An old white man in 1930s Alabama?" she said mockingly, waving her hand dismissively. "Girl, please."

"But Violet's right," he said, "He did try to teach Scout."

"White savior," she said. "Just another white man trying to save the day."

As he waited for more discussion, a knock at the door interrupted them.

"Hang tight," he said, wagging a finger at the students. "No phones."

He crossed the room and peered through the door's peephole. It was Maria Hidalgo, the school's new principal. He liked her; she had done an excellent job in her first year at the helm. Her face was tight, her lips pressed together in concern. She looked pale, the color of milk gone over. He opened the door for her. Behind her, other staff and administrators were streaming toward the other classrooms.

"Maria," he said, dispensing with the honorific. "What's wrong?"

Behind him, the inevitable buzz of students chatting had begun. Despite his admonishment, their phones would be out, which meant the rest of the class was shot. By the time he got them back on track, the class would be over.

"We're going into lockdown," she said. "Keep the kids in here and the door locked."

"What is it?"

"Don't know."

She continued down the hallway, leaving Tim perplexed as the door slowly swung shut. It was just a power outage, right? Or was it more? Had someone cut the power to the school? Was there a shooter out there right now? His desk. He would shove his desk against the door.

He turned back to the kids, all of whom had their faces in their phones. Several groups had formed as they showed their screens to one another.

"Someone help me with the desk," he said. "We're gonna barricade the door."

But no one was listening.

"Guys!"

"Mr. Whitaker?"

It was Joey Cauthorn, a tall, gangly kid with long, greasy black hair.

"What?"

"Our phones aren't working."

4

Lucy stood with her hands on her hips, struggling to process the events unfolding around her. They had made their way clear to the center of the large parking lot that serviced Union Station. Around them, dozens of people who had escaped the crash of Train 7894 milled about. The train had buckled at several points, the cars piling up on one another like a demolition derby. Some had sustained little damage, others were burning like hell, crumpled and charred.

To the northeast, the remains of the jetliner continued to burn merrily; a southerly breeze was pushing the black-gray smoke toward them, giving everything a hazy, washed-out look to it. The strange silence was pierced by the occasional sound of glass breaking and the distant rumble of explosions. No one seemed to know what to do or where to go. She admitted that she was one of them.

The most troubling development was that, other than a few D.C. police officers who had been on patrol nearby, there had been no serious emergency response to the train crash or the downed jetliner. It made no sense. She was standing in the middle of two mass casualty events and there was nary an ambulance or fire truck to be found. Maybe the emergency vehicles were on the far side of the crash, out of her line of sight. She put this concern on the back burner for the moment and turned to the second item that was blowing her mind. How could a plane have crashed at the same time as her train? What were the odds that a commercial airliner would go down within spitting distance of a train that had derailed?

"Hey!" she called out to a passing police officer. He was young, his face still bearing signs of teenage acne. If he was old enough to drink legally, it was just barely. His blond hair was buzzed close to the scalp.

"Ma'am?" he replied.

"What the hell's going on?"

"Not sure," he said, wiping his mouth with his hand. He looked pretty frightened when you got down to it. "Massive power failure."

"A power failure caused that plane to crash?"

"Ma'am, I really don't know what's going on."

Lucy tipped her head toward the girl and gestured for him to step away, out of earshot.

"This girl here, her grandmother died in the crash."

"Sorry to hear it."

"What can we do for her?" Lucy asked. "Help her get in touch with her family?"

"Gonna be honest with you, ma'am," he said. "There ain't a whole lot we can do. We've barely got any EMS or Fire here yet."

The officer tipped his cap and continued on his way. Her legs were unsteady underneath her; she felt like she was trapped in a terrible dream. Maybe she hadn't escaped the train at all, maybe she had died in the crash and this was the afterlife, this bizarre haunted version of Washington, D.C., an amalgamation of all the terrible things that could happen all happening at once.

Manny appeared to be as shell-shocked as she was; the girl—*what was her name again?*—Norah sat on the ground, her legs crisscrossed. She was scratching in the asphalt with a long piece of metal. The scritch-scritch of the metal on the blacktop was incredibly annoying.

"Can I have that?" Lucy asked, kneeling down next to her. "I don't want you to cut yourself."

"But I like it."

Lucy bit back a harsh reply. The girl had just experienced a massive trauma; the last thing she needed was Lucy, a perfect stranger, unloading on her, even if that stranger had saved her life.

"Sweetie, it's not a good idea to touch pieces from the train," she said. "The investigators will want all the pieces."

"Why?"

"So they can figure out why the train crashed."

Norah looked up at her with wide, brown eyes. She was quite striking.

"Okay."

She tossed the twisted shard of metal to the ground.

"Norah, where do you live?"

"I live with my grandmother," she replied.

"Do you live here in D.C.?"

"No, in Richmond."

"Richmond? That's where I live. We're basically neighbors."

The girl smiled broadly. Good. It was important to keep the girl calm, even as Lucy was finding it increasingly difficult to do so herself.

"What about your mom or dad?"

"My momma died when I was little," she replied. "I don't know my daddy."

"Anyone else? Granddad? Brothers or sisters?"

The girl shook her head.

Norah had no one. And Lucy couldn't leave this girl alone any more than she could leave her own child behind. She didn't know what looking after her would entail given the current situation; she would have to make it up as they went along. Improvisation. A critical skill for an emergency room nurse.

"Okay, Norah, I'm gonna look after you until we figure out what's going on," Lucy said gently. "You okay with that?"

Norah nodded.

"Great. We're gonna be a team and look out for each other."

She held out a fist; Norah bumped it with her own.

THE DEVASTATION WAS STAGGERING. Lucy, Norah, and Manny traversed the length of the wreckage, which ran nearly a quarter of a mile long; Lucy's jaw hung open at the sheer scope of the disaster. Bodies were scattered throughout the debris field. Other survivors staggered around in shock. It was by far the largest mass casualty event Lucy had ever seen. And still, no one came.

"Luce," Manny said, pointing ahead of them. "Look."

Off to their left, a young man was writhing and crying in pain, his leg pinned underneath a piece of the train's axle. He was one of dozens of badly injured people; they had to start somewhere.

"Let's help him," she said, accelerating to a jog.

By the time they reached him, the man was unconscious. To be honest, his lack of consciousness was a blessing; it spared him the agonizing pain the injury would have caused.

The heavy chunk of debris had turned the lower half of his leg into a bag of broken pottery. If he survived, and that was a big if, he would likely lose the leg.

"Help me get this off him." she said.

They stood side by side and leaned against the heavy

chunk of debris, driving their shoulders into it, but it was no use. It was just too heavy.

She knelt down to check on him. His breathing had slowed precipitously. A check of his pulse rendered more bad news. It was weak and thready. He was a good-looking kid, maybe in his mid-twenties. He was dressed in a pair of corduroy pants and a long-sleeve Ohio State t-shirt. His face was cut to hell, but the bleeding had largely stopped. She brushed his hair from his eyes and stroked his face gently. The man was dying and there was nothing she could do to stop it. She waited with him as his breathing slowed to a complete stop. A few moments later, his heart stopped. She did not try to resuscitate him, as the effort would have been futile and delayed the inevitable. She stood up and exchanged a knowing glance with Manny. There would be a lot of this today.

"Now what?" Manny asked.

"Let me think for a second," Lucy said, trying to get her bearings.

They had drawn close to Union Station itself, which appeared to be intact, despite a train car embedding itself in the outer shell of the building. Lucy debated venturing inside. There might be food and water and perhaps some official explanation about what the hell was going on. She did not hold out much hope for that, but it was possible. Every once in a while, you'd find someone who knew what they were doing. That said, she didn't love the idea of being enclosed with hundreds of people, many of whom would be frightened and panicked.

To the north lay Route 50, one of the region's primary arteries. Dead traffic clogged the highway in both directions. Dozens of vehicles had smashed into one another, giving this busy freeway the look of a demolition derby. Hundreds of people were out of their cars, chatting, many of them focused on the twin disasters before them, pointing, shrugging, confused.

Only then did it occur to her that whatever phenomenon had doomed her train and the downed airliner had also affected automobiles. As she stared at the steel braids of hundreds of motor vehicles, her brain locked up. It didn't seem possible. And yet here she was. And still no emergency response.

The smoke billowing from the remains of the downed airliner kept drawing her gaze. The odds anyone had survived were slim, and her heart shattered for the victims. At least she'd been lucky enough to be on terra firma when everything had gone sideways. That thought linked to another and then to another before her brain landed on the most important question of all. What had caused such a catastrophe? The odds that her train had derailed just as a perfectly good airplane had plunged from the sky without something connecting the two events were slim to none. Something had shorted out the electrical systems in their immediate vicinity.

Slowly, the last few minutes aboard the train began seeping back into the forefront of her mind. The man asking to borrow her charger. Her electronic reader going dark. Then the engineer losing control of the train.

She fell back on her medical training, running a differential diagnosis on the situation before her. What could have triggered such a widespread catastrophe? Her first suspect was a nuclear incident of some kind. Not long ago, she had watched a documentary about the risk posed by an act of nuclear terrorism – even if the blast was limited in scope, there was the possibility of a widespread failure of the power grid. A nuclear explosion in the atmosphere would be capable of generating an electromagnetic pulse powerful enough to render all technology in the blast zone useless.

But a nuclear blast seemed unlikely. The skies to the four points of the compass were clear, the sun shining down hard on them. There had been no flash of light, no mushroom cloud spreading its poison ash across the landscape. If there had been, the loss of technology would have been the least of their concerns.

A solar flare was another possibility. Back in 1998, a solar storm had wreaked havoc with the world's communication systems; that had been shortly before the ubiquitousness of the interconnected computer grid, before the world had gone online. She'd been a senior in high school; she remembered how helpless she felt, how utterly at the mercy of cosmic forces they all were.

That was more likely than a nuclear blast. With so many things dependent on sophisticated computer systems, and how the Internet was barely a thing back then, a repeat of the 1998 storm would be exponentially worse nowadays.

And people would panic.

"Are you all okay?"

A young black woman dressed in scrubs had approached them. She was short, powerfully built, and she wore her hair in a ponytail. An ID badge clipped to her waist identified her as Natalie Keaton, M.D. A heavy backpack hung from her shoulders.

"We were on the train," Norah piped up.

Keaton's eyes widened.

"You're one lucky young lady."

"This your daughter?" asked Natalie, turning her attention to Lucy.

"No, she was with her grandmother."

Then Lucy shook her head almost imperceptibly, enough that the young doctor got the message. She sighed.

Norah smiled a sad smile.

"My grandma died."

"Oh, honey, I am so sorry," she said. "But I'm glad you're okay."

"Thanks."

"My name is Doctor Keaton," she said. "Would it be okay if I check you out, make sure you're still good and strong? That was a big crash you came out of."

"Okay," Norah said.

"Any bleeding?" she asked as she palpated the girl's body, looking for signs of internal injury.

Norah shook her head. Lucy confirmed this for the physician. Keaton checked the Norah's eyes, mouth, arms, and legs. She pressed two fingers to Norah's wrist and counted off beats.

"Any pain in your head?"

"No."

"In your belly?"

Norah shook her head once again.

"Good," said the doctor.

Natalie squeezed Norah's shoulder reassuringly.

"Can I check your heartbeat?" asked Natalie.

She held up the stethoscope.

"This will let me listen to your heart."

Norah giggled at this. The doctor pressed the round disc up to Norah's chest and listened carefully for about thirty seconds.

"Everything sounds perfect," she said, pulling the earbuds out and hanging the stethoscope around her neck.

Natalie held up an index finger level with Norah's eyes.

"Follow my finger with your eyes."

Norah did so.

"Normally, I would check the pupils," she said. "But my flashlight isn't working."

Then she turned her attention to Lucy and Manny.

"How about you?" asked the doctor. "How are you all feeling?"

"Just banged up is all," Lucy said.

"Same," Manny said.

Natalie ran Lucy and Manny through her testing.

After a few minutes, she seemed satisfied that neither would collapse and die in front of her; this appeared to be the best she could hope for and all that she could offer under the circumstances.

Natalie threw a quick glance at the wreckage of the train.

"You're all really, really lucky," Natalie said.

"I know," Lucy said. "What the hell happened? I watched that plane go down."

"I work in that hospital across the way," she said, nodding over her shoulder toward the large complex just east of the train station. Her words tumbled out fast and clipped. A touch of a Boston accent.

"Right around lunchtime, everything went dark. Some kind of massive power failure."

She wiped sweat from her brow.

"Nothing's working," she said. "Nothing. Backup generators, redundant systems. The place went dark. In the OR, they were closing people up by candlelight. All the phones and computers went dead."

Lucy's heart skipped a beat as another puzzle piece fell into place. Things were even worse than she had suspected just a few minutes ago.

"When you said your flashlight wasn't working," Lucy said, her voice shaking, "I thought you meant the battery was just dead."

"No, I mean literally nothing is working."

This was a punch in the face.

"I guess that explains why no one's responded," Lucy said.

Such a disaster would push the region's emergency response system to its breaking point. The loss of life would be widespread.

"Yeah, we're doing the best we can here," she said, letting loose a chuckle that was half-laugh, half-grunt of disbelief. "An absolute nightmare."

"Any idea how widespread this is?" Lucy asked.

"No idea," she said. "Best we can tell, it's at least a couple miles in any direction. Not sure if that plane was taking off or on approach to Reagan. The airport's just across the river."

They stood in silence, taking another moment to process the disaster. The nurse inside Lucy stirred. A few years ago, it had been the coronavirus pandemic. It was why she had become a nurse. For events like these. All the training, all the patients, all the happy endings, the sad outcomes, the difficult discussions, the sleepless nights - all of it had been pointing toward this moment, in this place.

"Happy to pitch in," Lucy said, gesturing to Manny. "We're both E.R. nurses."

Keaton's face lit up.

"God, yes," said Natalie. "We've got more patients than we can handle."

"Norah, you okay if we stay and help some people?"

Norah nodded.

"You sure?" Lucy asked.

"Yes."

"Anything you can do," Natalie said. "Jump in anywhere."

The doctor dug into her backpack and removed a plastic bag of medical supplies: bandages, gauze, antibiotic cream, alcohol wipes, sample packets of ibuprofen.

"Listen," she said as she handed over the bag. "Help the ones you can. This is bad. Real bad."

Lucy nodded.

"Good luck," she said. "I'll swing back around and check on you when I can."

She moved on to triage other patients.

"You sure this is the best idea?" Manny said when the doctor had moved out of earshot.

"What do you mean?"

He held out his arms.

"I mean, look at this place," he said. "It's a disaster. It may not be safe here."

"I know it's a disaster," she said. "That's why we're staying."

"Listen, I have friends who live in Arlington," he said. "We could be there in a couple hours. Maybe it's localized. They might have power."

"Manny, these people need our help," she said. "And we might run into trouble out there too."

"But we'll be moving," he said. "And besides, I've got this."

He surreptitiously lifted his shirt, revealing a large handgun tucked in its holster.

Lucy tried hard not to roll her eyes but failed.

"Don't roll your eyes at me," he snapped. "You're gonna be happy I've got this. What are we gonna do when it gets dark?"

"Maybe this will all be over by the time it gets dark," Lucy said.

Manny laughed, a harsh snap of a chuckle.

"Does this look like it'll be over by dark?" he said, gesturing wildly.

She didn't reply, pressing her lips tightly together. He was right, but she didn't want to admit it, give him the satisfaction. Not that it mattered. Even if the power came back on in the next thirty seconds, there were still so many injured people to care for.

"Manny, this is our job," she said. She was a little surprised he was acting like this.

"Take a look around," she said. "This is what we are trying to do. This is why we became nurses."

His face cycled through a series of contortions before he finally sighed a big sigh.

"I know," he said softly. "I know."

5

There were so many victims.

"Stay close to me," Lucy said to Norah as they made their way toward the crash's epicenter.

Dozens of passengers had died in the crash, their bodies scattered amid the wreckage. A number had walked away with minor injuries. They were the lucky ones. Many others were seriously, even grievously wounded, and of those, a significant number would not survive.

Survivors drifted here and there, unsure of what to do. It was probably instinct to wait for help, for someone to come and do something, and perhaps that's what these people were doing. Small fires were burning everywhere and smoke clouded the air. Puddles of spilled fuel, twisted, charred metal, and personal belongings scattered six ways to Sunday.

"Okay," Norah said. Her voice was soft but firm. She was a tough kid, Lucy decided. Very tough. She reminded her of another young girl Lucy had known very well a long time ago.

The disaster was overwhelming in its scope. Lucy's shock must have been fading because with the clarity that even a little passage of time provided, the scene looked much worse. How they had survived, how anyone had survived, she would never know.

She set her sights on a single train car that had broken loose and came to rest in the middle of a side street bordering the train station. On its final journey, it had plowed through trees and cars and benches and tables and vestibules. Lucy hoped it had not hit any innocent bystanders, but that was probably a pipe dream. A derailment in such a congested area had probably killed scores of people who had not even been on the train.

"Sweetie, this is going to be rough," Lucy said to Norah. "But I can't leave you alone while I work. It's just too dangerous."

"It's okay," Norah said. "If I see something scary, I'll just close my eyes."

Lucy's heart broke. This was going to be a lot for all of them to digest, particularly for someone as young as Norah. But there wasn't much that could be done about that.

Her first patient was an elderly black man. He was sitting in between two large pieces of debris, staring blankly into space, his knees pulled toward his chest. But he was upright and conscious, and that put him far ahead of the curve right now.

"Sir," Lucy said. "Are you okay?"

He turned toward her, cradling a trembling right arm. His wrist bone looked out of place, his lower forearm resembling an inverted dinner fork. A silver fork fracture, they called it. She needed to reduce the fracture before he suffered permanent nerve and blood vessel damage.

"Got yourself a broken wrist there," she said.

He nodded. She knelt down next to him.

"We need to pop that wrist back into place," she said.

He glanced down at his arm and reared back suddenly as though he was seeing his injury for the first time.

"It's okay, it's okay," he muttered.

It was something patients often said as a mantra upon seeing their injuries for the first time; Lucy believed it was a function of the brain protecting itself from the reality of trauma.

"What's your name?"

"Albert," he said softly. He winced in pain.

"I'm Lucy."

He nodded at her but kept his eyes on his arm. The radius in his arm had broken and bent backwards, giving his wrist an almost alien look.

"Okay, Albert, this is gonna hurt, but we're gonna get through it. Can you stand up for me?"

He climbed to his feet slowly, staggering a bit as he

did so; Lucy grabbed him by his good arm to steady him. He took a deep breath as he set his feet underneath him.

"Ready?"

"Yes," he said firmly. His voice was deep and raspy.

"Manny," she said, "gently pin his arm to his side. Keep it as stable as you can."

It was a tricky maneuver she was contemplating, but the displaced bone needed to be reduced and shifted back into its normal position. She gripped his forearm tightly, and he flinched, understandably so.

"I'm gonna give your hand a good yank and shift the bone back into place, okay?"

"Got it," he said shakily.

"It's gonna hurt like hell," she said.

"Yeah, you've made that clear," he said, chuckling softly.

She struck while he was smiling, hoping the slight burst of endorphins would act as an anesthetic. While yanking hard at the base of his hand, she applied firm pressure to the bone and moved it back into place. He grunted once and then cursed loudly. Then it was done.

"We're done."

Albert examined her handiwork. His wrist looked normal again, albeit quite swollen.

"Wiggle your fingers for me," she requested.

He did so.

She tapped the tips of his fingers one at a time.

"You feel that?"

"Yep."

"Great," she said.

Manny handed her the medical tape just as she turned to ask for it. Sympatico. Always good when a health care team was in sync. She used the tape to splint the man's wrist as best as she could.

"This is a temporary fix, so see a doctor when you can," she said. "You'll probably need surgery on that."

"Thank you, ma'am."

The second victim was a heavyset man in his thirties. His name was Brett. He had been complaining of chest pains, and given the man's size and the trauma they had just endured, a cardiac event was not out of the question. She gave the man half an aspirin from the emergency kit the young doctor had given her. It would have to do. He also had a long laceration on his arm, which she bandaged after applying antibiotic cream.

The third was a young Latino boy, about the same age as Norah. He was with his father; neither of them spoke English, but Manny stepped in to translate. He had taken a blow to the temple and was complaining of a bad headache. He had a concussion, that was for certain, perhaps a subdural hematoma, but without a CT scan, there was no way to be sure. Lucy said a little prayer that the boy wouldn't collapse and die here.

And those were the easy ones.

Compound fractures, spinal injuries, and punctured lungs. Limbs shorn off. Terrible puncture wounds. She and Manny treated them with the most basic and primitive of battlefield medical protocols. A number of people were paralyzed; there was nothing to do for them but keep them immobile and hope that help arrived soon. As she worked, Lucy kept an eye on the horizon, hoping a bigger emergency response was on its way.

At some point, someone would come help, right?

Right?

The downed plane continued to burn like hell, making it impossible to get anywhere close to it. And there was more bad news. The flames were spreading to the commercial buildings, tongues of flame taking their licks of nearby fuel like a child tasting a lollipop.

Despite her and Manny's best efforts, victim after victim succumbed. They simply did not have the resources to treat such grievous injuries. After losing her third patient in a row, Lucy stopped for a break. She stood up and placed her hands in the small of her back, sighing at the crackle of her spine. Norah remained quiet but stayed close to Lucy as instructed. Manny had moved to care for patients at the north end of the parking lot, near the first three train cars.

"How are you holding up?" Lucy asked him.

He stood next to the body of a young woman, maybe in her early twenties. She had spiky purple hair and her earlobes were studded with earrings. Lucy focused on these attributes rather than the injury that had ended her life. Her arm had been torn off in the crash and she had bled out. Manny's belt, which Lucy recognized via his shiny Death Star belt buckle, was wrapped around her arm as a tourniquet. Manny's arms and shirt were soaked with blood.

"Okay, I guess," Manny replied, although he did not sound okay. His voice sounded robotic and far away. Not surprising. In their roles as trauma nurses, they saw death frequently; they were used to it. Death was like that guy in your poker game who usually played fairly but sometimes didn't. But this was more than they had ever seen. She grew increasingly horrified at the scale of it all, even as numbness to the scene crept in from the edges.

"You hearing anything new?" Manny asked. "We need some damn backup."

"I don't think anyone's coming," she replied. "Not anytime soon, at least. Nobody even responded to the plane crash. Not that it would've mattered."

Manny held a clenched fist to his lips as his eyes watered.

"What the hell is this, Luce?" he asked, his voice cracking. "I mean, what the hell is this?"

Lucy shook her head. She didn't know what to say. *What the hell was this, indeed*. She wanted to say something that would comfort him, that would comfort Norah, that would comfort Lucy herself, but she was coming up empty.

The three of them sat quietly near the body of the woman Manny could not save, watching the other doctors and nurses continue to work. After a bit, Lucy and Manny returned to the fray, helping those they could, comforting those they couldn't. As the afternoon wore on, the work wound down. Some of the patients had been moved inside the hospital, and, according to Natalie, they began discharging anyone who didn't need emergent medical care. Lucy couldn't imagine things were much better inside the dark and humid hospital.

Finally, the work was done. Lucy and Manny and the dozens of doctors and nurses from the hospital had treated every patient they could find. They had done a lot of work here, but she wasn't sure if she had moved the needle even a little. The ones who'd made it probably would have without her intervention.

Natalie was the last one working, providing CPR to a crash victim in the shade of an overturned passenger car. She refused to quit, desperately trying to massage life back into a dying heart. The look on her face was manic. Eventually though, her gyrations slowed to a halt and she plopped down onto her backside, pulling her legs close to her chest and locking her hands together.

Thunder rumbled overhead. The sky had taken the color of molten lead. A stiff breeze whispered around them. Dark skies as far west as the eye could see. Flashes of lightning embedded in the clouds like silvery threads. As if they didn't have enough to worry about. The approaching storm triggered a buzz of new activity. Hospital staff began moving additional patients inside. Many patients could not be moved and so would have to gut it out in the coming storm.

"Hey!" shouted a familiar voice.

Natalie jogged toward them, her white lab coat flapping behind her in the strengthening wind.

Lucy returned the wave.

"Thanks again for everything," she said. "It made a difference."

"I hope so," Lucy said. "Have you heard anything else about what happened?"

The woman's face darkened.

"We sent some folks out on a scouting mission."

"And?"

"It wasn't good," replied Natalie. "We sent people out in every direction, and it was the same everywhere. Nothing is working. And..."

"What?" Manny jumped in.

"One hasn't made it back yet."

Lucy ran her hands through her hair.

"Jesus, I'm sorry."

"I guess you guys aren't from around here," Natalie said.

"On our way to Richmond," Manny said.

"I wish I knew what to tell you," said Natalie. "Where to go. I'd offer you my place, but I live twenty miles from here."

"We can stay and help some more," Lucy said.

Natalie was shaking her head before Lucy even finished making the offer.

"No way," she said. "You'll need to take care of that little girl. She's gonna need rest, food, water. I wish I could offer you some supplies, but we're stretched thin as it is."

"Don't worry about it," Lucy replied. "Lotta folks in much worse shape than us."

"When this is over, either of you guys ever need a job, you come find me."

The physician hugged each of them before drifting back toward the hospital.

"You take care of these two jokers, you hear me?" she said to Norah.

"Yes, ma'am," replied Norah.

The crowd had thinned out. Those for whom D.C. had been their final destination had simply moved on, drifting away in dribs and drabs slowly over the past few hours. The growing desolation of the crash site came into focus. Lucy was still desperate for fresh information, some tidbit of news that would tell them the extent of this nightmare. But none was forthcoming. It was utterly maddening. How was she supposed to determine the correct course of action in the absence of any useful intelligence? They would be flying blind.

"Lucy," said Norah, her voice small and tight. She had been right at Lucy's side all afternoon, occasionally helping with the less critical patients. She had not looked away from the carnage; Lucy did not want to think about the emotional damage the girl was suffering. Well, that would be some psychiatrist's problem ten years down the road.

"You okay?" Lucy said, stretching her back.

"I'm scared of storms."

The girl was white as a sheet and her big eyes were wet with tears.

"It's not gonna hurt you," Lucy said, more dismissively than she intended. She wished she could pull her words back, she wished she had a full reservoir of patience to remind herself that kids could only be kids, no matter how dire the situation. Norah was doing the best she could.

The tears spilled over her eyes and ran down Norah's face. She stood with her arms by her sides, unswayed by Lucy's assessment of the situation.

"Can we go inside, please?"

Lucy chewed her lip for a moment.

"Please, please, please."

A flash of lightning, this one a crooked, splintery bolt pierced the sky.

One Mississippi, two Mississippi, three-

BOOM!

A huge clap of thunder that made even Lucy jump. The eye of the storm was just a couple of miles away now and truth be told, Lucy wasn't super jazzed to be outside now herself. Emma had not liked storms either. And, Lucy had to concede, the danger from lightning, while small, was not zero.

Fat raindrops began spattering the ground around them as the breeze continued to pick up. The lightning increased in frequency; the thunder was a constant rumble now, not much different from the sound of their train derailing.

"Okay," she said. "We'll wait it out inside."

Others had already started streaming toward the doors of the train station.

"Luce!" a voice called out.

Manny.

He was running as fast as his big frame would allow, waving his hand frantically. The rain had picked up considerably now, and she wanted to get inside before they were soaked to the bone. They had no clothes, no personal items. The explosion had consumed everything.

She pointed at the doors, gesturing for him to follow them. The station was jammed with people, listlessly moving about.

"Hold my hand tightly," Lucy said as she reached for the door handle.

The girl nodded.

"I won't let go."

6

The doors held fast.

Locked.

The storm intensified overhead. The thunder had become a constant guttural roar. Lightning flashed frequently overhead, the bones of bright white light fracturing the gloomy sky.

She banged on the doors as the rain soaked their clothes. There were two police officers standing on the other side of the glass with their backs to her. Certainly, they could hear her knocking on the door; then it hit her. They had locked the doors on purpose. She started banging harder, not worrying about whether she might break the glass. The doors were made of safety glass and would not break easily. They were probably bulletproof, another layer of defense against those that might wish train passengers harm.

One officer, a tall, stout man, kept glancing over his

shoulder toward Lucy, a hangdog look on his face. As though he wanted to let everyone in but that decision was above his paygrade. Finally, he turned around and faced her. A large crowd had formed behind her, everyone wanting to take shelter from the elements. The thunder boomed.

"No room in here," said the officer, making a throat-cutting gesture with his hand. His voice sounded muffled and garbled, like he was shouting underwater. "We're full!"

"You've got to let us in," said Lucy. "It's getting bad out here!"

The officer's partner, a petite woman, grabbed his elbow and turned him back around to face the inside of the station. The crowd's noise level grew from murmurs to a dull roar.

The mob pushed in close behind them, making for a tight fit. It was taking on a life of its own, something bigger and scarier than just a collection of people. The pulsing mass of humanity jostled them against the door. Elbows dug into her flank, pushed her against the door, almost pinning her to it.

"What do you want to do?" shouted Manny over the din.

The situation was becoming untenable. She wasn't even sure she wanted to get inside anymore. It would be dark, humid and chock full of panicked travelers far from home. Any valuable supplies likely had been cleaned out. She cupped her hands around her face and pressed them to the glass. Rainwater sluiced around her hands, down her arms, and into her shirt. Her wet clothes were sticking to her like glue. Without a fresh change of clothes, it was going to be a miserable night ahead.

A phalanx of new officers had joined the original pair, waving off the desperate crowd, which was getting antsier by the minute.

"Ow!" Norah exclaimed, rubbing the back of her head. She had probably caught a stray elbow.

"Let's get out of here," she said to Manny.

"Good idea," Manny said.

She took Norah by the hand again, and they edged their way along the glass doors until they found an opening at the crowd's perimeter. The rain was coming down heavily now, in sheets so thick that she could barely see two feet in front of her. It was so difficult to see that she almost missed it.

In fact, the only reason she saw it was because her ankle rolled underneath her as she hit the unexpectedly uneven ground. A narrow ramp to her right, leading toward a small door that had been propped open with a cinderblock. Ordinarily, this door would be closed, but perhaps someone had opened it to let in some fresh air given the failure of the HVAC system inside.

Even if they didn't plan to stay here very long, it would be nice to get out of the rain and dry their clothes for a bit. Maybe even take five damn minutes to catch their breath for the first time since the crash.

"Follow me," she said.

She kept an eye out as they made their way down the ramp; she didn't want to attract a large crowd lest they draw the ire of the train station security personnel, or worse, another mob. As they approached the doorway, the din inside the station became clear.

But the hot crackling boom of a nearby lightning strike disavowed her of any notion of remaining outdoors. Carefully, each of them stepped over the cinderblock and slipped inside the hot, humid train station. Inside, the rain sounded like static. It was hot and dank and likely to get worse. Without a functioning HVAC system, the station would warm quickly in the humid afternoon. And it was much darker than she expected. It shouldn't have been a surprise, but it was still disorienting. Electricity was something you took for granted. Light. There would always be something lighting the way. It was ingrained as deeply as baseball and apple pie. But not only was there no electricity, there were no flashlights, no backup lighting, no white beams shining from people's cell phones.

They huddled in a dark corner, near a supply closet and an employee bathroom. If not for the gloomy sliver of light coming in through the crack of the doorway, it would have been pitch black. The interior of the station buzzed loudly with conversation.

"You doing okay, kid?"

"I'm cold," she said.

"Let's see if we can get into the supply closet," Lucy said. "There might be some towels in there."

It was a standard door, flush with the doorjamb, not one of these high-security types.

"Manny, do you have your wallet on you?" Lucy asked.

"Yeah," he said, fishing it out of his pocket. He plucked a credit card from the billfold and handed it to her.

She winked at him but in the gloom, but she wasn't sure if he had seen her. She knelt down in front of the doorknob and slid the card in the narrow gap between the door frame and the strike plate. The latch popped free and the doorknob turned easily.

"Wow!" said Norah.

"Easy, peasy, lemon squeezy," Lucy said.

The door opened onto a small storage closet. A row of shelves took up half the room, about six feet by nine. The shelves were stocked with bottles of cleaning fluid, rags, rolls of toilet paper, and refill bottles of hand soap. She handed out the rags and the three of them spent the next ten minutes drying themselves off and squeegeeing as much water out of their clothes as possible.

"So what now, boss?" Manny asked. "Should we take a gander in the station?"

Lucy scratched the palm of her left hand with the thumbnail from her right as she considered Manny's query. There might not be much left in the way of food or water, but they could use some dry clothes. She didn't know what the next few hours held in store for them, but they would be far more difficult if they were wet and cold.

"I'll get us some clothes," she said.

"Are you gonna steal them?" Norah asked.

"Just borrowing them," Lucy said wryly. "I'll mail them a check."

"Can you get me one of those soft pretzels?" Manny asked.

Lucy laughed. The first light moment since the crash. It felt good to laugh. She hoped there would be more laughs today.

"You guys sit tight," she said. "I'll be back."

"You sure?" Manny asked.

"Yeah."

They agreed on a coded knock for her to use when she got back. She stepped into the hallway and pulled the door shut behind her. The corridor echoed with the loud snap of the lock.

THE DIM LIGHT of the day from the open door behind her was all she had to guide her journey down the long corridor. She kept close to the wall, which helped her maintain her heading. The farther she pulled away from the open door, the darker it got. The buzz of human activity grew in intensity with each passing step. Her heart was pounding; the experience was surreal. Ahead, the corridor brightened a bit, a rippling orange glow. Candlelight, if she had to guess. Probably a candle from one of those body shops. The whole place would smell like peppermint cinnamon before too long. She giggled at her own joke.

Another minute brought her to the end of the corridor; the wide open concourse rippled with the silhouettes of hundreds of people milling about. She blended quietly into the crowd, trying to take its pulse. The main concourse was calm; many people had set up little nests along the walls and in the corners in which to take refuge. Most of these travelers would be like her, en route to some other destination and so would have nowhere else to go in the city. Anyone for whom D.C. was the final destination would have long since taken their leave of this darkened way station. Many of the storefronts had shuttered, shielded by security gates. She did a loop of the lower level, but the trip was futile. There would be no supplies here.

She retreated to the supply closet and rapped on the door. Two quick knocks followed by three long ones. Manny opened the door.

"Struck out," she said. "The shopkeepers have locked everything down."

"So what do we do now?"

We'll wait until the storm dies down. Then we'll head into Arlington, see if your friends are willing to help us."

"Oh, trust me, she'll be willing to help," Manny said. "Angela owes me a favor."

"This is a pretty big favor," Lucy said.

"Lucky us," he said cryptically. "She owes me a big favor."

"How well do you know them?"

"I went to nursing school with them," he said. "They work at Fairfax General."

"Any idea how far it is?"

"Arlington is on the other side of the Potomac," he said. "Maybe eight or ten miles."

"Do you know exactly where they live?"

"Yeah," he said confidently. "Pretty sure."

"Will they be home?"

He shrugged his shoulders very dramatically.

"Guess we'll see!"

She sighed.

"It's close to the Ballston Metro station," he said. "I come up here a couple times a year to party with them."

Lucy was amused by the image of this forty-year-old man partying with twenty-something nurses. It was too much to contemplate, so she returned to the problems at hand. Manny seemed confident in their chances to secure lodging for the night, and so she did not press the issue. What she really wanted was information. She did not like being in the dark, literally or figuratively. She preferred to gather as much information as she could and rely on her own analytical skills to construct a picture of what had happened. It was why she watched breaking news stories as they happened rather than wait for a more accurate narrative of what had happened that came with hindsight.

Lucy did the math in her head. If they could manage three miles per hour, they would make it shortly after sunset, assuming they did not encounter any unforeseen obstacles. There was something ominous about abandoning the crash site; it was an admission that something was seriously wrong, something far beyond the tragedy of the train crash. As terrible as it was, trains did crash. It was inside the paradigm of what was normal. This was something else. It was beyond anything she had ever witnessed or contemplated. The worst part was that there was no way to know how widespread the effects were, which made it impossible to assess how much trouble they were in.

Norah had built a little nest with a stack of rags and towels. Her knees were pulled tight against her chest, and she had laid her head on top of her arms. Out of habit or out of desperation, perhaps a little of both, Lucy checked her phone again. The screen was still dark.

She went out into the corridor and sat with her back to the wall, her knees pulled up to her chest. The storm battered the area for a solid hour. The rain had doused the smoldering fires from the crashes; the air stank of smoke and rain and residue of the fuel fires. Steam and smoke swirled in the air. Eventually, the rain subsided as the storm cell dissolved, leaving behind a checkered sky of clouds and sun. A fresh breeze blew, the humidity broken. It was time to get moving.

"Norah, what do you think?" she asked. "Up for a walk?"

The girl shrugged her shoulders and nodded. Her arms were crossed tightly against her chest.

"Okay," she said. "Let's get moving."

She took Norah's hand in her own as they left the security of the station behind; they stepped outside and made their way up the ramp. The smoke from the two main crashes had largely dissipated in the rain. The crash site was largely deserted but for the dozens of dead bodies. The cars of the Acela lay where they had crashed. *Train Crash in Still Life.*

And no help was coming.

7

Tim Whitaker used the *Mockingbird* discussion to hold the class together, but after an hour, it became impossible to keep two dozen students focused on the material. He had quickly concluded that this was not an active shooter incident; there had been no gunfire, no screams, no police response. The obvious focus was the failure of their phones. It was quite the phenomenon to witness. For these kids, who lived their lives on the devices, it was like a drug-related withdrawal.

They quickly became antsy and restless, driven by the frustration of being unable to know everything now, now, now, of being unable to discuss the strange incident with their friends with their texts and memes and hashtags, of being forced to live in the moment, to live in the here and now. He didn't have the first damn clue what could cause such a catastrophic blackout. He willed the power to come back on, but it was not to be. Without air conditioning, the room grew increasingly gamey with the aroma of ripe teenagers whose deodorants and body sprays were failing them.

At some point, nature began making its inevitable call, and the students bold enough to do so used the crisis bucket to relieve themselves. It was as bad as it sounded. A five-gallon paint bucket partially filled with kitty litter. Some of the kids suffered from stage fright and were unable to relieve themselves, even with a tarp in place to provide privacy, no matter how much misery their full bladders were inflicting.

Once the amusement and novelty of the crisis bucket had worn off, tedium set in once more. He waited for a visit from up high, but none was forthcoming. He had not gone in search for answers, as the lockdown had not been lifted and he did not want to chance it. It was closing in on four o'clock, which Tim could tell by the angle of the sun, the way the light hit the corner of his desk just as the last bell sounded. But not today.

"Man, when are they gonna tell us what's going on?"

The question had come from Morris Klein, a big, strapping student on his way to Purdue in the fall on a football scholarship. He'd seen a few of Westerberg's football games; the kid absolutely obliterated onrushing defenders. Which was all a way of saying that if Morris decided to leave the classroom, there wasn't much Tim could do to stop him. He was a bright kid, and Tim had enjoyed having him in the class.

Tim folded his arms across his chest and blew out a confused sigh.

"Sit tight," he said. "I'm gonna go find out."

Morris helped him move his desk back to its original location and Tim left the classroom in search of answers. A small gaggle of teachers had congregated at the end of the hallway, near the staircase to the second floor. Holding court was the school resource officer, Penny Hill. Someone noticed his approach and waved him over frantically. As he drew closer, he identified the others in the group. Rodney Howard, a history teacher; Josephine Rocha, who taught Spanish; and Teresa Wood, who worked in the principal's office.

"Tim, you need to hear this," Josephine said in the sparkling accent that he would never admit to adoring. She turned her attention back to the officer.

"It's everywhere, and it's real bad," Officer Hill said. She was a squat woman, very businesslike, very fair, beloved by the kids. She treated all of them exactly the same, and for that, they respected her. Moreover, she was not prone to exaggeration.

"I walked down to the river, swept back this way," she went on. "Cars dead on the streets, planes fell right out the sky. I saw three planes down. Three big ones."

"How can that be?"

"No idea," she replied. "My walkie-talkie ain't working. Watches, radios, flashlights, nothing."

"This isn't good," he said. "Where's Hidalgo?"

"Speak of the devil," Josephine said, her attention

drawn to the staircase. Hidalgo was hustling down the stairs, her heels clacking on the steps.

"All teachers in the gym now," she snapped as she blew by them.

It took twenty minutes but eventually, nearly all the teachers had assembled in the large gymnasium. Hidalgo dispatched support staff to oversee the students in the classrooms with warnings to shelter in place under threat of serious disciplinary action. The faculty of about one hundred teachers gathered with the principal in the lower level bleachers of the gym. Sunlight streamed in through the windows, but it was quite gloomy. The teachers were ornery and in desperate search for answers.

Hidalgo clapped her hands loudly three times, which silenced the chit-chat.

"We still have no information about what's happening," she began, "other than this is a very widespread incident affecting most of the metro area. A number of kids have already been picked up by their parents or guardians. The rest I can't send home, as it's too dangerous."

"What about our own kids?" Teresa called out.

An echo of *yeahs* and *mm-hmmms* followed.

Teresa's kids were in elementary school; Tim didn't even want to think what kind of chaos those educators were dealing with. The scope of the disaster was just starting to settle in on him. The failure of the power grid would splinter families all over the area.

For once, Tim was happy he lived alone. That had been the status quo since the divorce from Madeline three years ago. No one to blame but himself for that one. The marriage had been in bad shape from the beginning, but he'd been the one to put the bullet in the back of its head. A lapse in judgment on a work trip with a teacher from Santa Fe. To this day, he didn't know why he'd done it. They'd been married four years and had no kids (her choice, not his). She would've granted him a divorce. He wasn't even sure why they had gotten married. They'd dated for a couple of years, and it seemed like the thing to do. It wasn't like those years had been starry-eyed, but he worked to convince himself otherwise.

But the woman in Santa Fe, Mary, had flirted with him at the bar and she had not cared that he was married, especially after he told her how awful his marriage was, that they hadn't even had sex in six months.

He felt horrible about the affair. He confessed as soon as he got home and he moved out that night. The divorce had been ugly and protracted and had cost him nearly ten thousand dollars that he didn't have. He was still paying the lawyer two hundred dollars a month to clear his balance.

But the key was that he was on his own. He didn't have anyone counting on him. His mother had died when he was in high school and he had been estranged from his father for twenty years. He didn't even know where the man lived. He had a brother in Denver he saw a couple times a year, a father to four kids. There were cousins and aunts and uncles, of course, scattered across the country and the world; he could help them no more than they could help him.

In short, no one was waiting on him; no one cared where he was.

"Don't get me wrong, I love these students, but mine have to come first."

"I know," Hidalgo said. "That's why I want to ask for volunteers who will stay for the duration of the crisis. If there are enough, then those of you with family obligations can leave."

Tim glanced around the room as he raised his hand. At least a dozen hands were in the air. A mixture of older teachers whose kids were grown and flown and several, like Tim, who didn't have kids at all. Hidalgo took a minute to count the outstretched hands. There were roughly a dozen volunteers. It would be enough. A wave of relief washed over Tim. He wanted these good people he'd worked with all these years to be with their families.

"Excellent," she said. "Those of you who wish to leave may do so."

Dozens of teachers began a slow procession out of the gymnasium.

"I'm sure the power will return in very short order," she said. "I look forward to seeing all of you very soon."

There were hugs and tears. Sixty-two teachers left the room that day. Within three months, half of them would be dead. Eventually, the exodus ended, leaving a skeleton crew of teachers with Hidalgo. The remaining thirteen funneled downward to the bottom row of bleachers.

"These kids are getting antsy," Tim said to the skeleton crew that remained. "We might be able to keep them for a night, but if it goes on much longer, it's gonna get hairy."

"We'll lock the doors," she said.

Tim laughed.

"These kids are smart," he said. "That won't hold them. Some might stay, but if someone decides to leave, there won't be much we can do to stop them."

There was no playbook for this kind of situation. They underwent crisis training every year, but this was not a scenario they had gamed.

"It doesn't matter," said Rodney. "I'm sure the power will come back soon."

"Let's hope it does," Tim said, not in the mood to debate the unknown. "Whenever it does, we're gonna have a hell of a mess to deal with. And it's not too much of a stretch to assume that a lot of the kids may have family or friends who died today. Us too."

This cast a dark pall over their meeting. No one had anything to add, so they decided to herd the students into the large cafeteria. He returned to his classroom where most of the students were waiting with bated breath. But not all of them. Some had already left, Morris Klein, the football player, among them.

"What are we supposed to do, Mr. Whitaker?" asked

one of the girls. The students had coalesced into a large group and so he could not identify who had spoken.

"We're gonna take shelter in the cafeteria," he said. "We'll release you to your parent or guardian when they get here."

He hoped his voice sounded firmer than it felt. It was strange the way the kids were acting. There was no defiance in them, more a current of fear. Their eyes were wide and their faces were shiny with sweat.

"What happened?"

"We don't know yet," he replied. "Let's get moving. Take your bags with you."

One by one, they made their way out of the classroom, joining a growing swarm of students flooding into the hallways en route to the cafeteria. As the classroom emptied, he sat at his desk to collect himself. The sunbeam etched its daily route across his desk, as it did every afternoon at this hour, moving from the lower left corner to the top right until it disappeared into the ether.

He went back out into the hallway and made his way down the long corridor. His footsteps were huge in the eerie silence of the high school building. He took the stairs at the north end of the building, climbing three flights through the stifling humidity to the roof access. He propped the door open with a cinderblock and stepped out onto the rooftop. He didn't want to risk getting locked out up here.

He made his way past the huge HVAC system to the edge of the rooftop, which gave him a clear view across the river and into the city. The sun was behind him. Normally, from this vantage point on a sunny day, the city was awash in a warm golden glow.

Today, however, was different. Today, the sun reflected off the heavy blankets of smoke wafting from the city.

8

L ucy was feeling better.

Just doing something was better than doing nothing. Better than waiting for others to dictate her fate. As they crossed the parking lot, Lucy's heart was racing in that way that indicated you were taking charge of your situation. She could see it in the others as well. A pep in their step, their heads lifted higher than they had been since the crash. It always felt good to take action.

They moved southwest around the perimeter of the station, passing a bank just beyond the westernmost tracks. It appeared abandoned. Here, they picked up 1st Street, which ran north and south parallel to the train station and fronted the Bureau of Labor & Statistics. This connected with Columbus Circle, a large roundabout on the south side of the station. A frozen traffic jam stretched out in either direction, dozens of vehicles wrecked or abandoned like a small child's forgotten toys. The drivers and passengers had clustered together in small groups, the way people did when united by a common struggle.

Train crash people went with train crash people.

Traffic jam people went with traffic jam people.

It was a strange phenomenon, a weird human dynamic. They would view Lucy and Manny as outsiders simply because they had not been part of the traffic jam. Once again, a sense of dread filled her. Uncharted waters.

Norah moved with purpose. She was holding it together for now, at least. She was pretty resilient. Or maybe she was just in shock. Kids were supposed to be resilient, they said. And maybe they were. But that didn't mean they didn't have their breaking point. Everyone did. And there was no way to know when she would reach hers.

She needed information. She couldn't stand not knowing anything about their predicament. And it would be good to collect data from various locations away from their personal ground zero.

She made eye contact with an African-American woman sitting on the edge of the rear cargo area of her Jeep Grand Cherokee, smoking a cigarette. Early thirties, well dressed. Lawyer or lobbyist, from the looks of it. She was quite striking, but she looked tired. There was a toddler in the back busy with a coloring book. Her Jeep was one of hundreds in this cord of traffic. The Day of a Million Fender Benders.

"Hey, you," the woman said. "You have any damn clue what's going on?"

"Not much," replied Lucy. "Only that anything electrical or battery powered shut down."

"Yeah, my car just died," the woman said. "Thought the engine had blown, so I was looking for a place to turn off when I noticed everyone else slowing down too. Damndest thing."

"What happens when you try to restart the car?"

"Nothing," she replied. "Key turns over. That's it. Nothing. Not even that clicking sound."

"You talk to these other folks?" Lucy asked, gesturing toward the other commuters.

"Same thing," she said. "Dead. Nothing."

"You see the plane crash?"

"Saw a couple."

The woman pointed toward the Potomac. The tail fin of a jetliner bobbed in the waves.

"Jesus," she muttered.

"The hell am I supposed to do? Christ, I live out in Ashburn."

Lucy did not know where Ashburn was, but she gathered it was not just around the corner.

"I'd be walking for two days. I'm just glad I had my kid with me. Had to bring him here today to see a specialist. He's on the spectrum. Not sure what I would've done if this happened while he was in day care."

The boy glanced up, sensing that his mother was talking about him. He was a cute kid. The conversation petered out like a river in a salt flat. There wasn't anything else for them to discuss. What else was there to say? They were all in a hell of a pinch. Yet Lucy couldn't help but wonder what this woman was going to do tonight. Sleep in her car? Take her chances on the road?

What were any of them going to do?

"Good luck," Lucy said.

"You too."

She nodded at her companions.

They threaded their way through the traffic, braided together by the various throughways crisscrossing this part of the city. Throngs of people drifted like snowbanks; most looked to be on their own or in very small groups like Lucy's. Workers on their lunch breaks, families touring the city on their vacations. People would be looking out for themselves and keeping to themselves.

They cut southwest across Massachusetts Avenue, following its bulge toward Louisiana Avenue. Louisiana continued southwest along the western edge of the Capitol grounds. In the distance, the Capitol dome shimmered in the late afternoon sun. The People's House, they called it. She wondered what was going on inside the bowels of that building. It was likely hardened against an EMP incident. The building would be closed for security concerns.

Locked tight as a drum. When the rubber hit the road, the politicians would think of themselves. She didn't want to believe that, and it probably wasn't true for all of them, but something happened to you when you went to Washington. You changed. Besides, she had some nerve thinking she was the first one to think of staking out the Capitol. Others would have reached the same conclusion she had.

Human nature being what it was, she suspected that would soon change if the power didn't kick back on in a couple hours. The scammers would come first. Simple cons at the beginning, like scammers getting people to turn over their phones to complete strangers because they had a trick to get the phone back on.

"Hey, Manny?"

"What?"

"Do you know what an electromagnetic pulse is?" she asked.

"No."

There was a nervous edge to his voice.

"Don't you read the news?"

"No, I hate the news. Work is bad news enough."

"Basically, it's a big burst of electromagnetic energy that gets released."

"Released by what?"

"Different things can cause it," she said. "Nuclear explosion in the atmosphere-"

"Aw hell no, someone nuked us?" he asked incredulously.

"Relax," she said. "That's just one possibility. And I don't think that's what happened. Skies are clear. No flash of light. And we're still alive."

"What if the nuke was far away?"

She considered the question, which was a good one.

"Yes, I suppose that's possible," she said. "And if that happened, well, there's nothing we can do. But other things can cause it. A solar flare. A freak magnetic storm. An EMP weapon."

"Oh, that sounds much better."

His sarcasm teetered on the edge of panic.

"Listen," she said. "Relax. We need to keep our heads together. You're a trauma nurse. You can deal with this."

"Okay," he said. "Okay. So an EMP did all this?"

"It's possible. A big enough EMP can fry pretty much all technology within a certain radius. That's why our train derailed, why those planes crashed. If it was a pulse, our trains, those planes turned into useless hunks of metal."

"For how long?"

"I don't know."

"It'll come back on, right?"

"Yes, I'm sure it'll come back on," she said as firmly as she could.

"Would this be everywhere?"

She didn't know. It was a scary question to contemplate. Even if it were limited to the continental United States, or even just to the East Coast, the loss of life would still be catastrophic. She had read that about ten thousand airplanes were in the air at any given moment, carrying about a million passengers. Anyone on a plane affected by the pulse would be dead now. That didn't even account for the mayhem unfolding on the ground.

"I don't know."

She took a deep breath and let it out slowly. Manny was getting on her nerves. He didn't mean it; he was freaked out and rightfully so. But she couldn't be his therapist right now.

"If I had to guess, it's localized around D.C. Obviously, it's always a target for terrorists. I'm sure help is on the way to the region from outside the affected area."

"But you don't know for sure."

"No, dammit, Manny, I don't know," she snapped, stopping dead in the street. "Why the hell would I know? I've been with you this whole time!"

He flushed like she'd slapped him in the face.

Good.

Get him on board.

She had freaked herself out just explaining it to him; the more she thought about it, the more certain she became that they'd just experienced an EMP attack. There was no other rational explanation. She could only hope that the effects were localized. She imagined armies of emergency responders en route to the D.C. area. She prayed for them, for their safety, but most of all, for them to get here pretty goddamned soon.

It had to be localized.

Because if it wasn't, then they were all in a lot of trouble.

"Sorry," he said without emotion.

Norah was watching them with great interest. Seeing her innocent face broke Lucy's feverish anger.

"No," Lucy said. "I'm sorry. I shouldn't have lost my cool."

"It's cool," Manny said. "This sucks."

Norah was on the point, but she was careful not to drift too far ahead.

"Norah?"

The girl looked back.

"Change of plans."

The girl nodded.

"What change of plans?" Manny asked.

"The Capitol is that way," she replied. "If there's any sort of emergency response underway, that could be ground zero."

"And we can find out what's going on?"

"Possibly," she said. "Don't get your hopes up though. We are talking about the government, you know."

"Right," Manny said, laughing one of his big laughs. The kind of infectious laugh that made you forget how annoying he could be. Underneath the insecurities of a forty-year-old man who desperately wished he was twenty-five, there was a pretty good man.

"We're gonna cut through this park up here on the left."

She remembered from a previous trip here that the spacious Capitol grounds were just on the far side of these wooded urban oases. They looked to be less congested than the streets, which were pulsing and swaying with thousands of people as clueless as they were. It wasn't a park exactly, but it would do.

A stand of trees rose up on the other side of Columbus Circle, about a city block's worth of foliage. Beyond it was green space, popular with city workers and tourists, a nice place to plop down with your lunch and a good book. That sounded pretty good right now.

There was a walkway cut into it from the street that looked promising. Lucy wasn't familiar with it, but she relished getting out of the bustle of the city and the growing buzz of panic around them. They zig-zagged across the street, through the broken traffic, and into the cool shade of the greenery.

It was distinctly gloomier in the cocoon of foliage, the trees heavy and full of leaves on this late spring afternoon. It reminded Lucy to keep an eye on the sun's course in the sky. They probably had three hours of daylight left. She was not looking forward to darkness falling across a city in panic.

She didn't expect much from this side quest to the Capitol, but she believed it would give them a good snapshot at the current state of affairs. It would give her an idea whether the chain of command was intact. The chain of command ensured that things kept moving in the right direction even while the world was going to shit. It was imperative that each cog in the machine believe the other cogs were operating, and as such, that the entire machine was working. And if one cog failed, the other cogs were holding firm.

That was why she wanted to see the Capitol. Her brothers and sisters in uniform guarding the building, keeping things safe. She wanted people to understand that. Most soldiers just wanted to keep the country safe. Sure, you had your loose cannons and your wackos, but soldiers were largely borne of a desire to serve. Seeing the Capitol would tell her if things were holding together. As a veteran, she understood the importance of the chain of command; on this day, perhaps more than any in the last century, it would be important for the country to have one.

Lucy heard voices up ahead. A small crowd had formed just where the trail curved due south, maybe half a dozen folks. The voices were charged and excitable and panicked. She kept a wide berth; entanglements with strangers were the last thing they needed right now. Not a single person knew anything more than she did right now. The risk of such encounters far outweighed the benefits. She took Norah by the hand as they passed the group.

"Hey!" a man called out as they swam by. "Any idea what's going on?"

"Nope, sorry," Lucy said without breaking stride.

"Fuck you, then!" replied the man angrily.

Norah pressed closer to Lucy as they picked up the pace. Lucy's nerves jangled; there was something upsetting about the exchange, brief and profane as it was. Her tours overseas had shown her how thin the line between order and chaos was, how fragile it really was. Lucy was by nature a pessimist. Life had made her that way; she wondered if a similar fate was in the offing here.

They emerged into an open glade lined with empty picnic tables and benches. D Street, also snarled with dead traffic, was the next cross street. A steady stream of people was making its way south. The crowd thickened like gravy, hundreds of people funneling toward the Capitol. There was fear and anxiety buzzing through the crowd, and she felt herself swept up in it. She was afraid and anxious too. Manny was just off her right hip, and Norah clung to her like an obedient puppy. Lucy took Norah's hand as they continued riding the wave. The girl's hand was warm and gripped Lucy's tightly.

She didn't know if this was a mob or a riot, and part of her didn't think they should be here at all, but there was nowhere else to go right now. There was nowhere to hide. Being plunged into such an unknown paradigm was disorienting. It had been hours since the event; information was still scarce. And as long as the lights stayed off, it would only grow scarcer with each passing hour. Better to get information now before the news devolved into rumor and myth.

The mobile crowd grew like an avalanche picking up snow down a mountainside. They crossed C Street, continuing northeast toward the iconic dome in the distance. Near Route 1, Lucy's rapidly growing group merged with another approaching from the southeast along New Jersey Avenue. The mob was now approaching a thousand people or more.

The pace was picking up now as the crowd zeroed in on its target. Lucy worried about the crowd trampling them. It did not look like the crowd, stretching, retracting, and expanding again, would give much thought to its individual components. The whole would be greater than the sum of its parts, greater than its parts. It would sweep across those parts entirely for the benefit of the whole.

Then she was running even though she didn't want to be running. Norah's hand was ensconced in hers. Behind her, Manny was huffing and puffing to keep up, but there was a look of determination on his face.

Next up was a massive pileup on Route 1, at least a dozen cars. A pickup had flipped over and landed on the roof of a sedan, which had slammed into a FedEx truck just ahead of it. A pair of cars had been sandwiched between the delivery truck and an eighteen-wheeler, which had jackknifed attempting to avoid the crash. Another half-dozen cars had run off the road and down an embankment, tearing up the steel guardrail in the process. There was a giant hole in the windshield of one of the sedans. It wouldn't have taken much to trigger a chain reaction accident. A sudden loss of control at fifty or sixty miles per hour and that would have been it. There had probably been thousands of similar crashes today. Unsurprisingly, there had been no emergency response to the crash.

My God, there were going to be so many dead and injured to deal with.

Then they were across Route 1 and onto the expansive grounds of the Capitol. Crowds of people were streaming toward the building from all directions. Lucy's stomach fluttered with panic. The size of the catastrophe was making her head spin. Just in this little corridor of America, tens of thousands of lives had been left at the mercy of the Pulse and countless others had been taken by it.

The crowd's momentum slowed considerably as they approached the Capitol like a spaceship decelerating outside a planet's orbit. The dome was less than a hundred yards away. Several thousand people circled the building.

National Guardsmen and Capitol police officers had taken posts at the top of the stairs guarding the entrance. All were armed; a few had drifted to the bottom of the stairs and were speaking to the crowd. This went on for a while as the crowd pulsed and breathed, stretched and contracted like a living thing. Lucy held Norah's hand tightly as the crowd jostled them to and fro; she was afraid she would lose Norah to the maw of the crowd.

"Ladies and gentlemen," a voice called out, booming across the grounds.

Silence dropped across the crowd like a heavy curtain. People were thirsty for information and this man was an oasis in the desert of this crazy ass day. Lucy craned her neck for a better view; a Capitol Police officer was addressing them via bullhorn.

He cleared his throat and then began to speak.

"Ladies and gentlemen," he repeated. "Thank you for coming here. This is the People's House. And I know you are here for answers. I will share with you what I can. At approximately eleven-forty-four a.m. Eastern Daylight

Time, the Washington, D.C. metropolitan area experienced a massive power failure. We know this is an unusual outage, and we want you to rest assured that we expect to have the power back on in just a few hours."

He lowered the bullhorn and for a few seconds, there was utter stillness and quiet across the crowd.

Then one woman shouted, "ARE YOU FREAKING KIDDING ME?"

Laughter washed over the audience; Lucy later remembered it as the last moment of normalcy they would have for a long time. People began shouting questions, one after the other, so many that they all got lost in the buzz of the crowd. Lucy was already regretting coming here. Hundreds of people were dead, possibly thousands, and this guy was treating it like it a thunderstorm had just passed through. Questions about the planes that had crashed, the phones that had stopped working, the cords of stalled traffic across the D.C. metro area.

Then things went to shit.

A group of folks rushed up the stairs, making a beeline for the soldiers guarding the main entrance to the Capitol building. The soldiers did not open fire just then, but with the high ground, they did not need to shoot anyone yet. They drove the butts of their weapons into the approaching midsections and chins of these scared and desperate people.

A veteran herself, Lucy was chilled to the core by what she had just seen. She could not believe it. She would never have believed in a million years that she would see American soldiers turn on those they were sworn to protect. Yes, they were defending themselves and they had used less than deadly force, but it was shocking all the same.

For a moment, the crowd was too stunned to do anything. All those times they had boycotted the NFL because of players kneeling during the anthem and this was how they were being repaid? Another phalanx of protestors charged the building, and they too were met with less than lethal force. But this time they were ready for the response and they quickly overwhelmed the small group of soldiers protecting that corner of the Capitol entrance.

"We need to get out of here," Lucy said to Manny.

"Agreed," he said, nodding his head firmly.

They backed their way through the crowd, the three of them clinging together like they were adrift at sea. Norah linked her arms with both of them, giving their pod some heft as they pushed through. Lucy glanced back in time to see a civilian brandishing one of the soldier's rifles. He aimed it skyward and squeezed off a burst. The gun kicked hard on him and rattled loose of his grip, falling to the concrete steps; it fired again, this time into the crowd.

They fled.

9

An hour of walking brought them to the Potomac River. The Theodore Roosevelt Memorial Bridge was just ahead, jammed with people streaming in both directions. They had walked west along Route 50 to get here, navigating a tapestry of stalled vehicles and throngs of people seeking leave of the city. It reminded her of 9/11, the pictures and footage of survivors pouring out of Manhattan across the bridges, the images fuzzy with smoke and soot of the collapsed towers. But seeing people moving in *both* directions here was disquieting. It suggested that the situation in Virginia was no better. She kept that sentiment to herself as they transitioned from the freeway to the bridge.

It was getting late fast. The sun was lower in the sky than she expected, as though even the big ball of light had had enough for today and was just eager to get to bed. Their shadows lengthened with each step across the bridge. A few owners had stayed with their vehicles, but most cars were abandoned. It was one thing, she supposed, to stay with your car on *terra firma*. It seemed to invite trouble to stay with it on a bridge. It didn't make a lot of sense, but Lucy could relate. She would have left her car as well.

Keeping to the edge of the bridge, they passed underneath the sign that guided the way into northern Virginia. The bridge flew over Roosevelt Island, part of the National Park System. Roosevelt Island was about ninety acres of unspoiled nature here in the middle of this megalopolis, free of automobile or bicycle traffic, veined with miles of trails and swamp and forest. To the north was the pedestrian footbridge, connecting from Arlington, providing access to the island. The setting sun glinted off the statue of Roosevelt.

It took thirty minutes to get across the bridge, but they made it across unscathed. They were in Virginia now. This made Lucy feel marginally better, like they had accomplished something. The freeways beyond and all the other bridges were clogged with dead vehicles in both directions, as far as the eye could see. A wave of refugees washed around and between the no-longer-rolling steel; from this distance they looked like ants navigating the tunnels of their colony.

"Focus," she whispered. "Focus."

One thing. Just focus on one thing. They had about sixteen different problems on their plate and she couldn't solve them all at once. Pick one thing and work on that. Food. Water. Shelter. These had to be their priorities. Forget about everything else. Forget about the mobs, forget about emergency responders, forget anyone coming to help. For the foreseeable future, it was just them.

"How you doing, guys?" Lucy asked.

"Good," said Manny.

"Norah?"

No response.

The girl was just off Lucy's hip, having clung close to her for the bulk of their flight from Union Station. Her face was flush, like she had just finished a hard workout.

"Norah?"

Her legs buckled underneath her and she went down hard. Lucy slid an arm around the girl's hip, just in time to soften her landing and prevent a bad situation becoming even worse. Lucy lay the girl down on the asphalt, tilting her head back slightly to keep her airway open. Lucy pressed two fingers to the girl's wrist. Her pulse was rapid but irregular, like a dozen worms were wriggling just under her skin. Her face was flush and damp with sweat. She wasn't unconscious, but she was in a deep stupor.

"Norah!" barked Lucy, clapping her hands in the girl's face.

The girl's eyes fluttered open, and her eyes rolled back in her head before bouncing back into place.

"You okay?"

"Yeah," she said softly.

Lucy ran through the different diagnoses that might have triggered Norah's collapse. Shock, hunger, dehydration, post-traumatic stress, an injury she might have missed, internal bleeding that she had sustained in the crash they had missed. Any one or more of these vectors might have been to blame.

She was awake, kind of, but she was still not all there. It looked like she was trying to speak. Her lips were moving, sticking together a bit.

She coughed, nodded.

Lucy did a quick assessment of the girl, checking her back, her neck, her arms and legs.

"I'm thirsty."

The girl was dehydrated. Lucy had forgotten to account for her age and smaller size; she would become dehydrated more quickly than an adult. Then an idea bloomed in Lucy's mind.

"Honey, this will sound weird, but I want you to suck on your shirt. It's wet from the rain and will give you some liquid you need. I promise you'll start feeling better."

"Ewwwww," she whispered.

Lucy did not add that the salt from her sweat would mix in with the rainwater and provide her with much-needed electrolytes. No need to gross the kid out even more. Norah complied.

As Norah suckled on her shirttail, Lucy checked their surroundings; they were on a pedestrian walkway paralleling the freeway. The exodus from the city continued; a never-ending flood of people continued its flight from the city. No one stopped to check on them, which didn't surprise her. Everything was in flux right now, and if there was ever a time for self-care, this was it. The world could be a cold place when it wanted to be. When it had to be. She didn't begrudge them these feelings.

Ahead was an exit ramp. To the east lay a commercial district. That would be their best bet to find a convenience store.

"Honey, can you walk?"

"I'll try," she whispered, but Lucy was doubtful. She was extremely weak.

She and Manny each took a shoulder and hoisted Norah to her feet, but it was like trying to balance two strands of overcooked spaghetti. Her muscles just weren't firing.

"Can you carry her?" Lucy asked Manny.

He was six feet tall and clocked in at well over two hundred pounds.

"You bet."

He hoisted her off the ground; he staggered a bit before finding his sea legs. She wrapped her legs around his back and rested her head on his beefy shoulder.

"You good, Norah?"

She nodded.

"Manny?"

"Yeah," he replied, already making his way toward the ramp. "I've eaten burritos bigger than this kid."

Norah chuckled softly.

A wave of affection for Manny washed over her. She believed in the old truism that adversity revealed character; it did not build it. And here, her slightly immature, party-hearty co-worker was stepping up to the plate in a way, if she were being honest, that she would not have expected.

"We can take turns," she said. "She's gonna get heavy quick, that much dead weight."

There was some traffic on the ramp, but not as much as on the main highway. A cooling breeze had picked up. It was refreshing after the heat and humidity of the day. As they walked, she once again assessed their situation, which was growing increasingly difficult to process.

Although she understood electromagnetic pulses as an academic matter, seeing the effect of one was something else entirely. Even if this proved to be a temporary setback, even if the power came back on in the next five minutes, the damage was done, and the damage had been catastrophic.

Their folly.

Their hubris.

They had placed all their eggs in the basket of technology, and they were now paying the price; that basket had fried their eggs something good. She pushed those thoughts away. There would be plenty of time to debate the socioeconomic ramifications of today's festivities. For now, Norah was her focus. Norah. A girl she didn't even know when she woke up this morning. Now, she held her life in her hands.

Lucy hoped they could find the girl's family in Richmond. She hoped the power came back on soon. It was a hell of a thing they'd all been through, but even more so for her. For all Lucy knew to the contrary, Norah was all by herself. Alone. She didn't want to think about what they would do if they couldn't find a safe place for her. So she didn't think about it. All she could do right now was keep her safe.

She would keep her safe.

~

EVENING.

The light had largely drained out of the sky, leaving behind an indigo twilight. And without the artificial light to which they were so accustomed, darkness was falling quickly. They were down at the bottom of the ramp now. Manny was fading with the extra load of Norah's weight. He was a big man, but he wasn't in very good shape. Every third or fourth step was accompanied by a grunt or a stagger.

"Sit down here," she said, gesturing to a concrete bollard at the bottom of the ramp. He did so without objection. He sat down slowly, careful not to jostle his precious cargo, and set his feet apart to stabilize himself.

The exit ramp connected with North Lynn Street, running north and south along the eastern edge of

Arlington. Just north of them lay a small commercial district, a mishmash of fast-food joints, gas stations and —*there!*—a convenience store.

Lucy checked on Norah. She was looking better. Not great, but better. At least she was conscious. Conscious was good. It meant the heart was pumping, blood was flowing, and that her lungs were leaching oxygen from the air and dumping it into her bloodstream.

"You want the gun?" asked Manny, holding it out in exactly the wrong fashion, the muzzle pointed at her rather than down.

"Do you know even know how to use this thing?" she asked, gently pushing the muzzle downward lest he inadvertently blow a hole in her chest.

"Dude, yeah."

"For real? When was the last time you were at the range?"

He looked at her sheepishly before looking away, cutting his eyes to the ground.

She huffed.

"Have you ever even been to the range?"

"Once."

"Christ, Manny," she said.

This was why she hated guns. Because they were not afforded the respect they deserved. Guns did not care. Mishandle one? Boom, your brains get splattered all across the kitchen counter. Forget to unload it? Bang, your three-year-old takes a bullet in the throat. It happened every day.

"Okay, pay attention."

After giving the gun a quick once over, she ran through some basic firearms training with him. She kept it as simple as she could, covering just enough to, if not guarantee, make it reasonably certain that he did not accidentally kill himself or Norah.

"Anyone tries to get at you, you aim at their chest. They get closer than six feet, you pull the trigger."

"Not the head?"

"Always the center mass," she said, tapping her breastbone. "They teach you to aim for the biggest possible target. You can do it."

That may well have been a lie. She didn't have the first damn clue whether Manny had it in him to take another life, even if he found himself with a reason to do so.

"Okay."

"You'll be fine," she said, already turning away from them.

She had to get moving, find this girl some water. It was getting very dark now, but her eyes were sharp and adjusting quickly. Eventually, though, the darkness would overwhelm the day, and her peepers would fail her. About a block west of the freeway ramp, she veered north and crossed the tarmac of a gas station. Foot traffic was heavy but orderly.

She carved a path around the gas station, around the far island of pumps. The store was set further back in a rectangular strip that included a nail salon and cell phone repair shop. As she approached the door, she gave the area a quick once-over, assessed what threats might lurk here, who might take interest in her entry. Before stepping inside, she checked her phone again, hoping to see the addictive glare shining back at her, but the screen remained dark. Any minute now, she told herself, any minute now, they would fix the damage to the grid.

The store was crowded, but it was reasonably calm. A handwritten sign taped to the counter informed customers that the store was taking cash only. Luckily, she still had a little cash in her wallet, money that she had planned to spend while sampling Philadelphia's nightlife at the nursing conference. Since she had turned in early every night, that money had remained safely in her wallet. The shelves were mostly empty, but there were a few sundry items of value, including a tube of summer sausage, plain crackers, a large bottle of water, and a few protein bars. She wanted to get more, but she only had twenty dollars.

As she waited in line, the queue's good behavior heartened her, although she was aware that was attributable to the forward momentum of civilized society. People were still acting civilized because they'd had no reason not to act otherwise yet. However, she did not know how long that would last. She gave it a day. The coronavirus pandemic, which had finally ended three years earlier after the development of an effective vaccine, came to mind. But since the outbreak had affected various parts of the country at different times and different intensities, the country had held together. The only events she could think of comparable to the Pulse were the destructive hurricanes that had ravaged the Gulf Coast states over the last two decades, sparking food and water shortages. But in those situations, emergency aid was at the ready just outside that narrow cone of devastation. They had time to prepare for those events. And the epicenters of those events were quite focused and narrow.

To be honest, she couldn't think of another situation quite like this in the country's history. It was like the devastation of 9/11 combined with the resource scarcity that followed a hurricane. Not a very good combination. If this didn't get remedied soon, this would be more like the scenes she had seen during her tours of duty overseas. Countries with no functioning governments, supply chains unable to meet the demand for food and water, no infrastructure to speak of.

The line was long and moving slowly. In the heat and humidity of the darkened store, the tensions rose. People were breathing heavily in the heat, shifting their weight from one foot to another. A man was arguing with the clerk. He was tall and thin and dressed in an expensive suit. He hadn't bothered to loosen his necktie.

"I don't have cash," he yelled. "I haven't eaten all day!"

"Sorry, sir," the cashier said in heavily accented English. "I can only accept cash."

"Screw you!"

The status quo was about to change again.

The man snatched the stick of beef jerky and a bag of Combos from the counter and bolted. This set off a panic. Within seconds, others had followed suit and began bolting for the door with their purloined loot. The clerk reached under the counter and pulled out a gun.

"Everyone out!" he yelled, waving it at his customers. "Do not take anything from the store!"

Shit.

There was no chance of getting a bite to eat unless she crossed that line between order and chaos.

Force majeure, she thought.

Acts of God.

Why she was relying on legal arcana just then to justify her dispensation of the rule of law she did not know. Around her, the orderly queue dissolved into chaos as customers, presumably all of them more or less a law-abiding bunch, turned into situational thieves.

As she made her way to the exit, a phantom arm emerged from the scrum, reaching for Lucy's bounty. She pulled her loot tightly to her chest and swung an elbow at her would-be assailant. She connected firmly with someone's hip bone. Grunts and shouts bubbled up from the cauldron of humanity that was rapidly reaching a boiling point.

Then a gunshot shattered the steady buzz of the crowd. In the acoustically challenged confines of the store, it was impossible to tell whether the clerk or a patron had fired. Someone screamed; a throng of customers streamed toward the exit, creating a bottleneck.

Well, that didn't take long. Barely six hours had passed since the outage and already, people were resorting to violence. Perhaps some weekend warrior, someone who'd carried a gun because it made him (and it would be a *him*, of that she had no doubt) feel like a big, strong man. Lucy herself knew damn well how to use a gun, but she hated them. That did not mean she did not respect them, and it did not mean she wanted them banned. She had three of her own back at home. But she had seen firsthand the damage they could do to the human body with no more effort than snapping one's fingers. Something that was a necessary evil was still evil.

A second gunshot split the air, followed by more screams. Lucy did not know if anyone had been hit, and she wasn't waiting around to find out. Without her own firepower, there was nothing more she could do. At that moment, she vowed she would not be unarmed for as long as this crisis endured.

She was on the last aisle, which was stocked with children's toys, beach gear, and greeting cards. A stuffed bear caught her eye. It was dressed in a bathing suit and had a stuffed snorkel attached to its mouth. It was cute and for a brief moment, it took her out of this surrealistic nightmare.

She grabbed it.

A third gunshot rang out behind her as she made it to the door, melding with the crowd fleeing the gunfire.

Before she knew it, the mob, bottlenecked at the door, swept her up. Bodies ebbed and flowed against her like the ocean with a strong current. Her heart throbbed up and down her chest, making it difficult to breathe. The bottleneck loosened as pieces of the mob broke off and fled into the darkness.

Pandemonium ensued; shoppers scattered through the store, scooping up anything that wasn't nailed down. Lucy took up a position in between a rack of postcards and the wall shelving of magazines and paperbacks. She was in the middle of the store, roughly twenty yards from the exit and the same distance from the rear.

She began edging her way toward the back, suspecting the store had another access point. She kept a wary eye on the crowd, most of which had flowed downriver to the exit. On the way, she passed a box of granola bars sitting under a rack of sunglasses, which she casually tucked under her arm.

God forgive her.

She made it to the back of the store, where she found a doorway marked *EMPLOYEES ONLY*. A quick check over her shoulder confirmed the coast was clear, everyone else looking the other way, and she quickly slipped through the door. This put her into the storeroom. She crossed through it quickly, deciding the risk of being caught was greater than the benefit of looking for additional supplies.

She ducked out into the alley behind the store; it was twenty feet wide, lined with large trash bins and swirling with loose garbage and debris. Lucy sprinted back to the rendezvous point, hoping no ill had befallen them. She did not think they would leave without her. The girl had latched onto her quickly, and Manny would want no part of caring for a kid by himself. He was a business nurse. Liked the work, liked the weird schedules, liked the pay for thirty-six hours a week, but he did not take his work home.

There!

They were in a bus stop vestibule. Manny was on his feet, prowling, patrolling, working to keep people out of their little safe zone. She jogged over to them, waving her hand as she approached.

"Luce!" he called out when he saw her.

The girl jumped out of her seat and threw her arms around Lucy's waist. Her little body trembled.

"I was so scared," she said. "I thought they were gonna hurt us."

Lucy was perplexed.

"What happened?" she said, looking over to Manny. She noticed a red welt on his face that hadn't been there earlier.

"Got jumped," he said softly. "They got the gun."

Lucy's heart sank.

"Oh, Manny," she said. "Are you okay?"

"Yeah," he said quickly. He seemed deeply embarrassed. "I could've gotten it back, but I didn't want to leave Norah by herself."

She allowed him this fiction; she was just happy he

hadn't gotten them killed. They would just have to make do without the gun.

"Where did you go?" asked the girl.

"I had to get you a snack," Lucy said, pulling the box out for them to see.

Lucy tore open the box and handed a bar to the girl. She gobbled it down, finally content and oblivious to the world around her.

"I thought you didn't carry cash," said Manny.

She replied to him with a glare, nothing more.

He held her gaze for a few seconds before he caught her drift. His eyebrows jumped.

"Daaaaamn, Luce!"

"Let's move while we eat," she said. "It's not real safe here."

She did not want anyone else to discover their stash of granola bars. Her gut was still swirling with bad mojo. She did not know how long it had been since the crash, but it had been several hours. The sun was peeking through the still-significant cloud cover and had begun its final approach toward sunset. Darkness was not far away.

Things would start unraveling quickly now. The scene at the market would be replayed over and over across the affected areas. Supplies would dwindle quickly. And that's when things would really start to get scary. People were panicked, and panicked people made bad, even violent, decisions. Decisions they never would have made if it had been an ordinary day in May and the world was humming along as it always had. And being so far from home put them at a massive disadvantage. While others could stockpile or simply have the good fortune of being at home, they would have to travel light, even if they found a bumper crop of supplies.

"What happened in there?" asked Manny. "We heard a gunshot."

"It's getting rough."

Manny sighed.

"Hey, Norah, I got you something," said Lucy, holding up the stuffed bear.

The girl looked up from her granola bar and squealed with excitement when she saw it.

She hugged it tightly.

"We need to get moving again."

10

It was completely dark now. There was no denying it, no sliver of light in the sky remaining to guide their way. If Lucy had to guess, it was around nine o'clock. Ten hours until sunrise. They had made it about three miles into Virginia, crossing through a residential district in Arlington. Candles were burning in many windows now, which they used as beacons. Lucy was working hard to maintain a westerly heading, lest they get turned around and end up back at the river. A cold front had moved in, blanketing the area with a thick layer of clouds. They streamed across the sky like sailboats on a starry sea.

Norah was still riding on Manny's shoulders, still cuddling with her bear. It had made more of a difference than Lucy expected. Norah was quiet but alert. The adrenaline from the shock of the crash and its aftermath was fading, and soon, she would have to deal with the fact that her grandmother had died and that she was all alone. Then the work of healing would begin.

But first came the hard part. Norah was in the in-between phase, in the gap between the trauma and the posttraumatic stress that was sure to follow. Everyone was strong until they had a moment to think about what had just happened.

Another hour of walking brought them to the corner of Wilson Boulevard and North Rhodes Street, where they broke for a snack at an abandoned outdoor café. Lucy's feet throbbed; she was glad she was wearing tennis shoes. She said a little prayer for all the women who'd had to endure the last eight hours in heels. Just another way women got screwed.

The break helped; Norah grew perkier with each bite of her granola bar. After polishing off a second one, she cuddled happily with her bear. Manny clearly needed the break. But as they recharged their batteries, Lucy felt a tickle of discomfort, like someone was watching them. She didn't know why she felt like that, as there were hundreds of people out here, moving in all directions, north, south, east, and west. It was an instinct she'd honed while in the Army. A skill that had proven particularly useful while she was overseas. Something out of place, an overly friendly local, some innocent harbinger of things about to go side-ways. She scanned the crowds, but she didn't see anything; her body continued to buzz with alarm. They rested for another ten minutes before setting off once more.

A small neighborhood lay on the far side of the café. She debated walking up one of the stoops and knocking him the door, seeing if any of these families would offer them a little charity here in their hour of need. But she was just kidding herself. Those lucky enough to have made it home today would be hunkering down. The Pulse had hit in the middle of the workday, just a few weeks before the unofficial start of summer. People would have been out and about, grabbing lunch, running errands. Once it became clear that this was no ordinary outage, tens of thousands would've simply hoofed it home. The last thing they'd want right now would be strangers darkening their doors.

No.

They were on their own.

And she couldn't shake the feeling that someone had an eye on them.

"Manny," she said softly.

"Yeah?"

"Keep your eyes open."

"What's wrong?"

"Just do it," she said firmly but gently.

"Okay. "

She wished desperately for the gun, imagining how good it would feel in her hand. She was a good shot, a fact evident from her earliest days in the Army. She was one of the best in her class. It was quite a contradiction. She hated what guns could do, but she understood that they were necessary. And as long as they were necessary, she wanted to be the very best at using them.

"Manny, you take the lead," she said. "Norah, you walk in between us."

Lucy brought up the rear as they made their way down a wide sidewalk fronting well-maintained lawns. Majestic maples and oaks lined the curb to their left. In the summertime, the full branches reached over the street and met their mirrors from the other side of the boulevard.

Lucy kept her head on a swivel as they trekked westward, suspicious of every shadow and shimmer of candlelight from the windows.

"Freeze," she hissed at her compatriots.

They had stopped in front of a tall hedgerow fronting an adorable little Cape Cod. Lucy's internal warning system was blaring now. *Red alert, red alert.* She thought she had spotted movement between the trees, but she couldn't be sure. This concerned her more than anything. Anyone this skilled at moving so stealthily in the dark would be a powerful adversary indeed.

Keeping her eye on their rear flank, she edged forward and took the point. She checked behind each tree as they passed it, expecting an ambush. Norah must have picked up on Lucy's concern. The girl's breathing had become rapid and shallow. Manny picked her up and swung her onto his shoulders. This seemed to calm her down.

But they were still in danger; of this, Lucy was certain.

She did not know how their hunter had been able to track them so stealthily. But they were past that now. Before continuing westward, she checked behind the hedgerow, the perfect spot from which to launch an attack. But it was clear. The silvery moon shimmering down illuminated the end of the street about a hundred yards distant. Beyond lay a line of trees.

They were very exposed here; she hoped this imminent change in the terrain would give them cover and the chance to lose their pursuer. Although she couldn't see anything, someone was out there. She could feel it in her bones.

"Nobody there," Manny whispered.

She looked directly at him and pressed a single index finger to her lips. After another fifty yards or so, the road terminated in a cul-de-sac buttressed by a small park. They passed one more house, dark and foreboding on this late spring evening, before reaching the park entrance. A thick copse of trees guarded the front of the park, which itself was ringed by a narrow walking trail.

They could not turn back. They'd be walking right into the teeth of an ambush.

"Just so you know," she called out loudly, "I've got a gun. And I know how to use it."

A harsh whisper in reply.

"Good," hissed a frightening sounding voice. "Very good."

"Leave us alone!" barked Manny. His voice cracked and he did not sound as intimidating as he was hoping.

Her stomach fluttered.

As though they didn't have enough to worry about.

"Are you hungry?"

No reply.

"We have food," she said.

"I know you do," said the voice. Every word passed over the filter of a grotesque whisper.

"We're happy to share."

"We don't want to share your food," said the voice. "We want all of it."

"I don't want to hurt you," Lucy said. "But if you get any closer, I will kill you."

And she would have, given the chance. Lucy had never been afraid to do what had to be done. That was the function of her Army training. She was a tool to implement policy decided by others. It was not her place to question that policy. Because that's how the military worked, that's how the military had to work. Otherwise, the entire chain of command would break down.

But it wasn't just that. They were all nearing a line that could not be uncrossed. Like the scene back at the convenience store. The line between order and chaos was dissolving. She didn't know what the voice wanted. For all she knew, this was some kind of cruel prank. But she had to treat it like a mortal threat. There was no margin for error. She would be a tool to execute the policy of keeping them alive.

"Why don't you go into the woods?" the voice said. "We can have lots of fun in the woods."

"You don't know me," she said.

"But I want to be your friend," said the voice.

"I've got a better idea," Lucy said.

"Is that right?"

"It is," Lucy said.

"And what is this idea?"

"That you kiss my ass."

She grabbed Manny by the shoulder.

"Run," she snapped at him. He lumbered onto the trail.

"Can you run?" Lucy asked Norah.

She nodded vigorously, stutter stepping into a jog and then a run, breaking ahead of her two older companions. The disembodied voice had frightened Norah badly, and she was more than willing to take her chances in the dark wood. She gave Manny a hard shove in the back before falling in behind them. In the trees, the moonlight faded like a theater going dark at the end of the night.

"Move, move!" Lucy hissed, keeping her head on the swivel. She saw no one behind them, but the unnatural sounds of pursuers crashing through the brush were loud.

She cursed the loss of the gun. Without it, they were naked, at the mercy of anyone who might try to exploit them. If only Manny hadn't been so careless. *Dammit!* Maybe he should stay behind and face-off their pursuers. After all, it was his fault that they couldn't properly defend themselves. It was a terrible thing to think, but she thought it anyway.

Norah's young eyes were sharp and she did a good job negotiating the trail ahead. The trail was well maintained, approximately four feet wide, just enough room for two lanes of foot or bicycle traffic. She had no idea where the trail led, unfamiliar with this part of the city. If it curled back south, they would abandon the trail and take their chances in the woods. Ideally, that would prevent their pursuers from executing a pinscher maneuver and boxing them in on the trail.

She debated abandoning their supplies on the trail; it might eliminate the threat. But there was no guarantee that these bandits would simply let them be. Because they had entered a period of lawlessness, and there was nothing to stop these people from doing whatever they wanted with impunity. All manner of terrible crimes would go unpunished. After the power came back, there would be too much to damage on a global scale to repair to worry about any single atrocity.

"Hold up," she said.

Manny and Norah froze. Lucy primed her ears, listening, listening. The sounds of pursuit had faded. But they were not off the hook, not by a long shot; the bandits had changed their strategy. They had to get off the trail.

"On my shoulders," Lucy whispered to Norah.

She knelt down while the girl climbed up on her shoulders like a baby monkey. Norah clipped her feet around Lucy's waist and crossed her arms around Lucy's neck; mercifully, she was careful not to squeeze Lucy's throat too tightly.

Before setting off, she scanned the trees again, but it was like looking for a needle in a sea of needles. It was bad enough that they were being hunted like dogs; worse was that they were flying blind. She did not know the terrain at all, and the absence of virtually any ambient light made things exponentially more difficult. The leaves rustled in the late spring breeze, the branches rocking ever so slightly, just enough to make every branch resemble the arm of a would-be killer. The only plan of attack was to stay one step ahead of these jerks until they lost them.

How had it come to this? In a normal world, she would be home by now after the long train ride from Philly, curled up with her pup on the couch, watching television and eating Chinese food.

Her dog.

Oreo.

He was the sweetest pup one could imagine. Although at five years old, he wasn't really a pup anymore. His fur was black but for a white stripe running down his chest, and he had the most pitiful eyes you could imagine. He weighed about sixty pounds, but he fancied himself a lapdog. As soon as she settled on her couch, there he was, curled up next to her, resting his massive head on her knee. Her brother was looking after him as Jack often did when she was away.

She pushed Oreo and Jack out of her mind. She couldn't worry about him right now.

"Follow me," she said to Manny.

They plunged into the brush. It was slow going through the trees, every step an adventure. Manny followed on her right hip, keeping a hand on her shoulder. Every few steps, Lucy tossed a glance over her shoulder, still unable to lay eyes on the threat.

A few minutes later, the forest thinned out, and Lucy's heart soared. They were almost through the woods. They broke through the tree line and into a clearing; across the way lay a small office park, quiet and deserted. The parking lot was still full of cars, but the complex felt desolate. In the foreground was a squat building about four stories high. Beyond it were two larger buildings, but in the dark, it was difficult to ascertain their precise dimensions. To the left, a multi-level parking deck rose into the sky.

She tapped Manny on the arm and gestured toward the office building. He nodded his understanding. They took a moment to catch their breath and then sprinted for the complex. She was gambling on the prospect that the building's doors were unlocked because of the power failure. Her heart pounded, and her chest and her lungs burned from the extra weight she was carrying. Sweat slicked her exhausted body. She ran and ran, her quads vibrating and burning, making a beeline for the faint outline of a door near the corner of the building.

Behind her, Manny huffed and puffed as he kept pace. They entered the building, falling into near total darkness. They were in a long corridor now, bracketed at the end by a second doorway, barely illuminated by the spill of moonlight like liquid silver. Ominously, the door was closed.

"Can I set you down a second?" Lucy asked Norah, lowering her to the ground. Immediately, sharp relief flooded through her. The girl wasn't particularly heavy, but carrying her was no picnic. She stepped gingerly toward the door. She reached for the lever, her heart in her throat.

Locked.

Dammit.

A crunch of gravel behind her.

Lucy froze with her hands on her hips, breathing heavily as a result of their desperate sprint through the woods. Behind her, Manny gagged and then threw up. It had probably been a while since his last all-out sprint.

"It was a good run there, friendos."

Her shoulders sagged.

"Turn around slow."

She turned around slowly.

Lucy's eyes had adjusted to the darkness. There were three of them standing just outside the door. She couldn't make out the leader's precise facial features, but he was young, his hair buzzed close to his head. Behind him were two more young adults, a man with long hair tied back in a ponytail and a girl, thin and petite with short-cropped hair. He was leveling a handgun at them.

"Sorry for all the scares," the man said, waving the gun around. He was just a boy, really. "We really just want your pack. We know you've got food."

Lucy sensed an opening. Maybe they wouldn't be entirely unreasonable.

"Look, we're from out of town," she said. "This is all we have."

"Hey, same here!" the boy said. "Just passing through looking for work. Hell of a time to be away from home."

The girl laughed. It was the laugh that distressed her more than anything else. Jesus, were people truly this callous? The power had been out for less than twelve hours, for God's sake. Which meant this girl was just normally this awful. It was her default setting.

"What if we split it with you?" Lucy said. "This will get us all through to tomorrow, and by then, this will all be over."

"No," the leader said. "All of it."

"Please," she said.

"Hand it over," he said. "I won't ask again."

Lucy's shoulders sagged as she determined there was no escape. No chance of a heroic takedown of their assailants. They weren't armed, and they were badly outnumbered. For the time being, this was how it was. Kill or be killed. She couldn't let this happen again.

Lucy shimmied the pack from her back and tossed it into the four-foot gap between the two groups. She mourned the loss of the supplies. She had lied to the man. She really did not believe everything would be up and running the next day. Next week? Maybe. But she was starting to have her doubts.

"Grab it," the man said to the girl.

She stepped forward, retrieved the pack, and retreated to the safety of her group.

"Sorry guys," the leader said. "Really."

The trio backed out of the building, leaving Lucy, Manny, and Norah all alone.

Norah had fallen quiet since the encounter with the three bandits. There wasn't much life in her face; she ambled with the gait of someone on a forced death march. They were still moving east, having edged their way south back to Arlington Boulevard, a typically busy artery running along the spine of the county. Hundreds of cars sat inert like an automobile graveyard.

"Everything okay, Norah?"

She shivered.

"I'm really scared," the girl said. "When is the power gonna come back on?"

"I'm sure it'll come back on soon."

The girl began to cry. Strangely, Lucy felt a weight lifted from her shoulders. She had been waiting for this moment since the train exploded. Norah had been through a lot. It was good to get these emotions out. You had to process them or they would pull you down. This was, to date, the worst, most traumatic day of this girl's life. She wouldn't get over it in a few hours.

"I miss my grandma," she said in between waves of tears.

Then Manny jumped in.

"It'll be okay," Manny said. "Of course you're gonna miss her, you're never going to see her again."

Lucy sighed with exasperation as the girl began to cry harder. She knew what Manny was trying to say, but he had said it in the worst possible way. Now the girl was openly sobbing, her mournful wails echoing along the freeway, the sounds bouncing off the abandoned vehicles.

"Come here," Lucy said, opening her arms.

Norah flung herself into Lucy's embrace, wrapping her skinny arms around Lucy's waist. The child was in full meltdown.

"Shhhh," she said over and over into the girl's ear.

But Norah was inconsolable. Lucy could not calm her down, and worse, they were drawing attention from people around them, which was the last thing they needed. She wanted to be invisible. Standing out would be a sign of weakness and invite predators even more dangerous than the reckless teenagers that had already gotten the best of her.

"Sorry, Lucy," said Manny. "I was just trying to help."

"Yeah, maybe think next time," she snapped.

His face fell like a poorly constructed cake. Norah was

trying to talk, but with her face pressed up against Lucy's chest, her words were muffled.

"What are you trying to say, sweetie?"

"What's gonna happen to me?"

"I'm not sure about that right now," she said, regretting it instantly.

Dammit, Lucy thought. She had just teed off on Manny for doing the same thing. Now she had set the girl off too. She glanced at Manny, who looked back at her with some smug satisfaction. He was wise enough to keep any snarky comments to himself.

At that moment, Norah wrenched free of Lucy's grip and took off down the sidewalk.

"Shit," she muttered. She bolted after her, desperate to keep Norah in her sights. In the inky blackness, it would be easy to lose her. She could just make out Norah's silhouette about twenty yards ahead. A pit formed in Lucy's stomach; the girl was fast. This was no joke. If she didn't catch her soon, she might lose her for good.

No, she thought. She wasn't going to lose her.

She wasn't going to lose her like she had lost Emma.

LUCY HAD MET Nate Prescott at a friend's thirtieth birthday party. He had been very forward; they had met in line at the bar, and by the time she had a glass of wine in her hand, she had already given him her number. The relationship wasn't super serious yet, more like *almost* serious. They were in that transition to *de facto* cohabitation. It was that cloudy part of a new relationship when you realize you haven't been home in a week and you've got a toothbrush and a few changes of clothes at their place. Dinner together had become a default thing rather than something that had to be set up in advance.

She had been careful, dutifully taking her birth control pills every morning when she woke up, just before she stepped in the shower. She never forgot her pill, or at least she thought she never forgot it. She didn't even remember the onset of the morning sickness; one day, it occurred to her that she'd been feeling nauseated for a few days, maybe as long as a week. Initially, she wrote it off to a stomach bug. Stomach viruses could linger for weeks, and in her work as an emergency room nurse, there was no shortage of disease vectors.

One night after work, she heated up a microwave dinner and fired up an old movie, a funny flick about a TV personality who discovers she's pregnant after a one-night stand with a lovable pothead. Lucy sat up with a start, and after a detour to the bathroom to puke yet again, she made a beeline for the drugstore down the street where she bought half a dozen pregnancy tests.

Every one of them was positive.

She was twenty-six years old and had been working as a nurse for almost five years. Her time in the Army had come and gone. She loved her job and she was having the time of her life; she believed she had been born to become a nurse.

Becoming pregnant was the last thing on her mind. In fact, she was already thinking of breaking things off with Nate. Being with him felt like a chore, like an obligation. And if that was how she felt now, it wasn't going to get any better. But she didn't want to give up just yet. He was a decent guy, better than most of the ones she dated. She didn't know if she was in love with him, not knowing what it meant to be in love with someone. Still, it was not a very good sign to be having these thoughts so early. That said, braided with the fear and shock of the sudden development was a current of pure joy.

Then Nate, good sport that he was, made the decision for her. She asked him to meet her for breakfast, which, looking back, was dumb, because the aroma of sizzling bacon sent her running for the bathroom the moment she had set foot in the diner. They ordered coffee, decaf for her, and he sat there with a bored look on his face, frequently checking his phone.

"I'm pregnant," she said.

He looked up from his phone. Awesome. Something interesting enough to pull his attention from his Twitter feed. She felt like she was in one of those romantic comedies. Sitting in a diner, looking across at the unsuspecting father-to-be.

"Fuck," he snapped, the obscenity like a slap in her face.

It wasn't the response she was hoping for, but she let

it slide, giving him a minute to process her news. Unfortunately, things had gone downhill from there.

"I don't want a damn kid," he said, drumming his fingers against the peeling tabletop.

Tears began streaming down her face. She hated crying in front of him, especially given the hate and contempt in his eyes. Worse, she didn't even know why she was crying.

"You're gonna get rid of it, right?"

You're gonna get rid of it.

You are.

You.

He was treating it like an irregularly shaped mole that needed removal. She sat mute. She hadn't even thought that far ahead. She just wanted to get him on the same page with her. She had assumed the best about him; she understood now that was a mistake.

Was there such a thing as a romantic horror movie? Because she felt like she was living one right now.

"Aren't you on the pill?" he said grudgingly.

"Yes, I'm on the pill," she said much more loudly than she needed to. Loud enough to draw the attention of other diners. She had never been one to make a scene, but if ever there was a time for one, it was now.

"Keep your damn voice down," he snapped.

"Don't tell me to keep my voice down."

He wilted under her retort, a new piece of evidence proving the kind of man Nate Prescott really was. Part of her, and not a small one, was tempted to have this baby just to spite this man. Of course, she immediately hated herself for thinking it, but that didn't mean she hadn't thought it.

"I thought it was foolproof."

"I guess it didn't work," she went on. "Maybe you can have one of your fancy lawyer buddies sue the birth control pill company for me."

They sat in silence for a while. He nibbled at his omelet, and Lucy, in the throes of morning sickness, sipped at her decaf. The waitress quickly refilled their coffees and left their check at the edge of the table.

"So you are gonna get rid of it, right?" he repeated.

That again.

The unconscionable asshole.

Nate loved one thing in life and that thing was Nate.

She didn't answer. He wiped his mouth with his napkin, set it down, threw a twenty on the table, and left. He didn't say goodbye, as though this was a conversation to be picked up later.

But they never did.

She waited for him to call, she waited for him to call, and she waited for him to call. He never did. Then she had to decide whether to walk down that road fraught with so much emotion and anger and partisanship and science and religion. And, in the end, she decided to have the baby. She hadn't meant for the pregnancy to happen, but it had happened, the same way that it happened to billions of other women throughout history. She was no better than them, she was no worse than them. Many had been good mothers, many had been average, and many had been terrible. She did not know which one she would be, but she wanted to find out. And she didn't have any good reason not to have the baby. Because she had loved the baby as soon as the plus sign had shimmered in the oval window of the pregnancy test stick.

To be fair, her parents were not thrilled that their only daughter had become pregnant outside of wedlock, but they got over that pretty quickly, excited at the prospect of becoming grandparents. The pregnancy had been unremarkable, as the doctor had noted in her chart, which was a strange thing to say because once the pregnancy ended and seven pounds, eight ounces of Emma Goodwin came rushing into the world, something very remarkable happened to Lucy Goodwin's life.

She ran into Nate once more at the grocery store when Emma was about three months old; Emma was at her grandparents', and so he had not seen his infant daughter. He was engaged to a dermatologist named Diana and was preparing to move to Boston with her. She never saw him again. And that was fine with her.

Because it had been wonderful. Emma was an easy baby. Happy and so full of life that it was nearly bursting from her. As though life itself was not grand enough to contain her, not big enough to absorb the love she had to offer the world. The eight weeks of maternity leave were the best; just the two of them getting to know one another. Emma wasn't a great sleeper, and breastfeeding had gone poorly, which was its own nightmare, but other than that, it was magic.

And when she went back to work after those eight glorious weeks, she put Emma in the hospital's employee day care center; she felt guilty, of course, as all working mothers did, but Emma was in good hands. Just being able to see her once or twice during her shift kept her engine running.

Yep, those first few years with her had been the best.

Then Emma had gotten sick.

"NORAH!" screamed Lucy, no longer caring about drawing attention to themselves.

There!

Norah materialized in a sliver of moonlight bouncing off a building at the corner of the block. It was a small, squat building fronting a clear-cut tract of land. As she drew closer, Lucy could see it was a football field at the edge of a high school campus. Lucy picked up the pace, hoping that Manny would be able to keep up.

"I'm headed for that building," she called out.

Manny was huffing, his cheeks puffed and his wheezing loud in the still night as he tried to keep up.

"You go," he said. "I'll catch up."

Luckily, a chain-link fence had slowed Norah down. It was a good-sized fence, roughly twelve feet in height. Norah's struggle to scale it would hopefully give Lucy enough time to close the gap between them. But Norah was more limber than Lucy gave her credit for. She scaled the fence with ease and was on the other side of it before Lucy could halve the distance between them.

Lucy pushed herself harder, covering the last fifty yards in the blink of an eye. It had been a long time since she had sprinted this way, and it felt like her heart might explode in her chest. She slammed into the fence, grabbed the links with her fingers, and began climbing. Norah was already on her way back down the far side.

"Norah, please wait," Lucy said between ragged gasps.

"Leave me alone!" the girl wailed.

Halfway down the fence, Norah jumped to the ground and bolted again. Lucy cleared the top of the fence, shimmied down a few feet, and then chanced the leap to the ground from a height twice her own. The fence twanged and rippled as it absorbed the energy of her leap. She hit the ground hard, her legs buckling underneath. Pain shot through her lower body, but her balance held. She broke back into a run without stopping for a systems check; if her body was going to fail her, she would find out soon enough.

Norah was running diagonally across the football field toward a parking lot to the south. Lucy turned on her jets now, finally starting to chew up the distance between herself and Norah. The girl was fast, but she was starting to run out of steam. She was running on pure terror and grief, those spigots close to running dry.

Then they were within sight of the high school's main

building. The moon slipped behind a cloud, and Lucy lost track of Norah as she cleared the end zone. Then the cloud slipped past; Norah had traversed the field and was now near an open door on the western perimeter of the school building.

Lucy didn't think the girl would go inside the dark, cavernous building alone, but Norah quickly proved her wrong. Norah disappeared through the doorway, the building swallowing her up like an unexpected snack.

She was gone.

12

L ucy continued giving chase, making it to the door about thirty seconds behind Norah. Using a bit of caution that was absent during Norah's flight into the building, Lucy checked her surroundings once more. There was nobody around; the quiet was immense. Then she stepped inside.

It was the smell she noticed first. Lucy had been out of high school for more than twenty years, but the tangy aroma of sweat and body spray and the woodsy vanilla of old textbooks took her back. It was like stepping out of a time machine right into eleventh-grade English class. She couldn't even remember the last time she'd been inside a high school, but in the darkened corridor, she could hear Mr. Sale droning on about Hester Prynne and the scarlet A on her dress. What letter did they put on unwed mothers? What would they say about the fate that had befallen this unwed mother? Probably that it had been God's will.

Get it together, Goodwin. Miles to go before you sleep.

Lucy was in a long corridor stretching interminably into the darkness, well beyond her range of sight. A bit of moonlight dribbling in the doorway dimly illuminated the hallway and the random ordinary of a high school. Bulletin boards and rows of lockers as far as the eye could see. She edged her way close to the wall, using it to navigate the corridor. This was a big school, and she had no idea how she was going to find Norah.

After a few moments, she came to the first doorway; perhaps a classroom or an administrative office. She jiggled the door handle, but it was locked. This was a positive development. Locked doors would cut down on the number of places where Norah could hide.

"Norah," she called out. Her voice echoed off the walls and came back to her like a ghostly replay.

She primed her ears for a reply but received none.

She wondered how the blackout had played out here. It would've been difficult for the staff to keep hundreds of high school students in place, especially with their own families to worry about. Still, it wouldn't surprise her to discover stragglers here, kids and teachers with no place to go. Once again, she was reminded that there was no playbook for this.

If only the girl hadn't run. They could be working to address the catastrophic loss of their supplies. That problem was not going to go away, after all. That was how crises worked—you picked one problem and fixed it, and then you moved on to the next problem and the next problem until the crisis was resolved. And as long as they were in the dark, it was reasonable to believe that more crises lay ahead. But adding unnecessary crises to your plate was how you got yourself killed.

She was in total darkness now, beyond the reach of the moon's thin beams. Up was down, no beginning, no end. She couldn't even see her hand in front of her face. Night-vision goggles would have been handy; then she remembered that battery-powered goggles probably wouldn't have worked either. What a nightmare.

Another minute or two of floating in darkness brought Lucy to an intersection. She held her breath, trying to distill any sound that might lead her to Norah, but the place was as silent as a tomb. The immense quiet was incredibly distressing. Their powered, technological world had had its own soundtrack, a buzz that lived in the background of your life. Power lines, telephone wires, cellular phone towers, airplanes, trains, automobiles, all of these working together to generate the backdrop of the twenty-first-century civilization. Now, it was gone.

What were they going to do?

A wave of panic washed over her; her breathing came in shallow pants and her heart was racing. She hoped that they could recover from this without too much collateral damage. Today alone would have been catastrophic, a 9/11, a coronavirus pandemic a hundred times over. Everything would be just scrambled to shit right now.

A sound broke Lucy out of her depressing assessment

of the state of the world. A rattling sound, like someone jiggling a doorknob farther down the corridor to her left. She put her left hand to the wall and continued deeper into the building's interior. She wished she had Manny's lighter with her. Amazing how the simplest of things could become so valuable in times of crisis and how much difficulty their absence could create.

With no way to mark her travel, she began counting her steps. Every fifty steps, she paused and checked the other side of the hallway for any room that she might have missed. After two hundred steps, she paused. She heard nothing at first, but after a few seconds, she picked up the faintest of murmurs. It could've been the wind, a draft, or someone whispering. She froze a bit longer, hoping to distill more information from this newest discovery.

She counted off fifty more steps before pausing again; the murmurs had grown louder. Definitely conversation. A chill ran through her body, like someone had dragged an ice cube straight down her spine. There was no telling what kind of people or trouble Norah might have found in these dark hallways. She continued flying blind down the corridor. Even with her improving night vision, it was almost impossible to see anything.

After another forty steps, she reached a significant break in the wall. Further exploration revealed a set of double doors. A small pane of glass was set into each of them. An orange glow flickered right at the edge of Lucy's line of sight through the glass panes. This was probably the gymnasium or lunchroom. The voices were louder here. She chanced a glance through the glass. Dozens of people were inside, most sitting at tables, others drifting in small groups. Most looked young, but there were a few adults. The ones who had stayed behind. Candles sat on each table, giving the place a positively medieval look.

Lucy opened the door and stepped inside, drawing the attention of a heavier set woman near the door.

"Who are you?" she said, loudly enough to draw the attention of others nearby. They fell silent, which caused a ripple effect throughout the rest of the cafeteria. Quickly, the place became quiet.

"I'm looking for a little girl," Lucy said. "Her name is Norah. She panicked and ran away from us."

The woman held up a finger.

"Wait here."

She drifted into the crowd, which lost interest in Lucy and resumed its cacophony. A number of board games and card games were underway. A few kids snacked on fruit and pudding cups. In the soft glow of the dozens of candles, it looked downright cozy. A far cry from the utter chaos of the last eight hours. She tipped her hat to these teachers for keeping their shit together and their students safe. Not just safe, but calm. Even if the kids hadn't ventured outside, they would know that something was seriously wrong.

The woman returned with a companion, a tall, broad-chested man. He wore typical teacher garb: khakis and a button-down Oxford shirt. His sleeves were rolled up.

The male high school teacher starter pack. If he'd been wearing a tie earlier in the day, he had since shed it.

"You the one looking for the girl?" he asked.

"I'm Lucy," she said. "You've met Norah, I take it."

She held out her hand.

"I'm Tim. Tim Whitaker," he said as they shook.

"Nice to meet you."

"This is Debbie," he said, nodding toward his companion.

Lucy nodded her head in greeting.

"Is she here?"

"She's here."

Lucy let out a long sigh of relief.

"Can I see her?"

"You family?"

"No, our train crashed. At Union Station. She was with her grandmother. She didn't make it."

His shoulders sagged at this news.

"Sorry to hear it."

"Thanks."

"So you've been out there?"

"Yeah."

"Is it bad? We've gotten some reports from parents who came to get their kids, but almost all the students live within a couple of miles of the school."

She took a deep breath and let it out slowly.

"It's really bad."

"Did the planes really just crash?"

"Yeah," Lucy said, the image of that doomed jetliner

burned on her brain. "Yeah, they just fell out of the sky. Never seen anything like it."

The woman clapped her hand to her mouth.

A loud booming voice in the hallway caught her attention.

"Lucy!"

It was Manny.

"The other member of our little traveling party," she said. "Let me grab him."

She retreated into the hallway and found him stumbling in the dark.

"I found her," she said. "She's safe."

"Good," he said, a bit sarcastically. "I can wring her little neck now."

"Give her a break. She's had a terrible day."

"Yeah, it's been a real picnic for me."

She ignored the quip and led him by the arm back to the lunchroom. His head jerked around as he noted how many people were here.

A commotion erupted in the middle of the cafeteria; two boys jawed at one another, each in the other's face. Then one took a swing, the other ducked, followed by him plowing into the other's midsection. The two tumbled to the ground in a braid of chaos and violence.

Before Lucy could blink, Tim had plunged headfirst into the fight. The boys continued swinging at each other in their inelegant brawl, but after a moment, Tim emerged from the fracas like a phoenix, holding each boy by the collar. They were big boys, but at Tim's mercy, they seemed small.

"Knock this shit off!" he bellowed.

The boom of his voice froze the two combatants, froze the entire room. He flung each of them loose, sending each staggering backwards.

"Haven't we got enough to deal with?" he snapped. "Not enough that we're in the middle of some catastrophe, you've got to pull this nonsense? It's not enough?"

The two boys withered in the face of their teacher's admonishment.

"Go on, get out of my face," he said. "I better not see you within twenty feet of each other.

The boys retreated into the safety of the crowd, careful to distance themselves.

"Sorry about that," Tim said, returning to the conversation.

"No problem," she said. "Can I see her now?"

Tim looked at his coworker.

"Let me talk to her for a second," he said. "She's had a good scare."

Lucy nodded. He wanted to confirm that Lucy was on the up and up; she could respect that. As he went to talk to Norah, the students returned to their tables, back to their board games. Things were calm again. They seemed uninterested in drawing Tim's ire a second time. It was clear they respected him.

A few minutes later, Tim returned with Norah by his side.

"Hey," she said sheepishly.

"Are you okay?"

"Yes. I'm sorry I ran."

"It's okay."

Lucy breathed a sigh of relief. Norah was safe.

"You folks hungry?"

"God, yes," Manny said.

"Wait here."

13

L ucy sat down next to Norah. A small candle sat on a glass base, flickering in the darkness. It smelled like pine. Norah lay her head down in her arms on the table. She must have been exhausted. Lucy understood why Norah had run. This was unlike anything they had experienced. The plug had been pulled on all of them. They were truly cut off from one another. She had no more idea what had become of her extended family than she did the man on the moon. Their world had shrunk down to whatever you could see, hear, or touch in front of you. No more, no less.

They were all living in shadows.

"Can we talk for a second?" she said, curling her arm around the girl's shoulder and squeezing her gently. Norah didn't lean into the hug, but she did not pull away. She shrugged.

"I'm going to make sure that you are safe," said Lucy. "You trust me?"

Lucy made sure her voice was firm but not harsh. Norah looked up at her, her eyes puffy and her cheeks stained with tears. She was breathing as though she might break down at any moment again.

"I know this is a scary time, but I am not scared. And I promise to keep you safe."

"Okay," whispered Norah.

"Can you do something for me?" Lucy asked.

Norah nodded almost imperceptibly.

"We've got a long way to go," Lucy said. "And the three of us have to work together to get there. If you get scared, you come to me first. It's not safe for you to run off like that. Right, Manny?"

"Definitely, dude," he replied.

"How old are you anyway?" Lucy asked. "Thirteen, fourteen years old?"

"No, I'm only eleven," exclaimed Norah, giggling.

"Eleven?" Lucy replied, feigning surprise.

Norah nodded.

"Well, you are very mature for someone who's only eleven," she said. "As grown-up as you act, I would've thought you were a teenager. Believe me, you're being braver than I bet a lot of grownups are right now. You're a tough kid."

This delighted Norah immensely, as Lucy suspected it would. Now was the time to inject her with confidence; Lord knew they would need it. She stood up and yawned.

Fatigue was setting in. This was the first moment of peace any of them had had since the crash. Her body ached. Hints of soreness from the crash began rippling in her back and ribs like storm clouds appearing on radar.

Tim returned with a bag of snacks and drinks. A mixture of apples, bananas, pudding cups, candy bars, and potato chips. He also offered them each a chocolate milk. Lucy pushed one to Norah and encouraged her to drink one immediately. People didn't understand how quickly dehydration could set in and make a mess of you. They dug in; Lucy reminded them not to eat too quickly, lest they develop a stomachache or end up running for a toilet.

"Also brought you some Tylenol and ibuprofen from the nurse's office," he said. "I figured you may have some bumps and bruises from the crash."

"Thanks," Lucy said, chasing down two tablets with a swallow of energy drink. She gave Norah one tablet.

She was starving; she hadn't partaken of the granola bars before they were stolen, so she hadn't eaten in twenty-four hours, not since grabbing a slice of pizza from a little Italian place down the street from her hotel the night before. If she had known what today would turn into, she would've eaten the whole pie.

Tim sat with them, his arms folded on the table.

"Where you folks from?"

"Richmond," Manny said. "We were on our way back from Philly."

"And everything just lost power?"

"Everything."

He ran his hands across his face, shook his head in disbelief.

"How is that possible?"

Lucy told him her theory about the electromagnetic pulse. He shook his head in disbelief.

"What are you gonna do now?" he asked.

"I've got a friend that lives not far from here," Manny said. "We went to nursing school together."

"You guys are nurses?"

"Yeah," Manny said. "I used to work with her at Fairfax General."

"I used to date a nurse who worked there," Tim said.

"Really? What's her name?"

"Angela Hughes."

"Angela Hughes?" repeated Manny. "Long black hair, blue eyes?"

Tim nodded.

"That's her. You know her?"

"That's who we're on our way to see."

"Oh. Small world."

"And you dated her?"

"She was the school nurse here a few months before taking the job at the hospital," Tim said. "That's how we met. Wow. It really is a small world. Anyway, we didn't go out very long. Just a couple months. She had an ex that was never quite out of the picture."

"Eric," both men said simultaneously.

"This is crazy," Manny said. "What are the odds?"

"Anyway, I really thought we had something, but I don't think she ever got over him."

Lucy liked Tim. He had a quiet, disarming, almost naïve way about him. He did not seem to have an agenda. When Norah had landed on his doorstep, he had helped her. When Lucy and Manny had followed, he had helped them. He had been a helper. Perhaps he did not fully grasp the gravity of the situation outside.

"Nice of you to stay with the kids," said Lucy.

"Someone had to. I'm single, no kids. Easy call. Most of the faculty and staff had families to think about, try and track down. Besides, I live about twenty miles from here. Too far to chance it tonight."

"Wow, that far?" Lucy asked.

"Yeah, most high school teachers don't make enough to afford a place in this school district. Not without a healthy second income, that is. Anyway, you all are welcome to stay here."

"Nah," said Manny. "It's not far to Angela's."

A burst of laughter erupted from one of the tables. One of the kids was putting on some kind of show and had her friends in stitches. It made Lucy's heart ache. Emma would have been a little younger than them now, had she not been taken so quickly.

EMMA WAS eight years old when she got sick. It had started uneventfully like these things often did. She hadn't been feeling well for about a week. It was almost Christmas, a season that Emma ordinarily loved, so when she hadn't been up to shopping for a tree, much less decorating one, Lucy knew she wasn't feeling well. The symptoms weren't particularly troubling. General fatigue, a low-grade fever, symptoms consistent with a virus. Initially, Lucy had written it off to a bug that Emma had picked up at daycare. Nothing like a couple years in daycare to turbo boost your kid's immune system and your personal guilt. It was that time of year. She didn't think it was the flu, as Emma had gotten her shot in early November. Vaccines were sacrosanct to Lucy. Emma was afraid of needles, so they always got them together.

But as Emma's illness dragged into its second week, Lucy decided to get her checked out. She just didn't seem to be getting any better. Her appetite was virtually nonexistent, her glands were swollen, and she was complaining of increasing joint pain. After palpating her stomach, the doctor noted that her spleen was slightly enlarged. Her white blood cell count was extremely elevated. The suddenly anxious pediatrician ordered a bone marrow biopsy and a spinal tap; that was when Lucy got nervous.

Emma was too young to understand what was happening. All she knew was that she didn't feel well. Then the waiting began. That was the worst time, living on the edge of two different realities and waiting for fate to shove them into one or the other. Schrodinger's Lab Tests. Lucy was not a religious woman, but she prayed to God all the same. She didn't know why she did it; it was just something to do. She didn't even know if it made her feel any better. Emma began sleeping next to her mommy, a special treat Lucy rarely allowed. She lay awake watching her daughter sleep the sleep of the righteous and the innocent, her stuffed duck tucked just so under her arm.

Not Emma. Please, not Emma.

The pediatrician's office called on a Thursday morning. The time stamp to end all time stamps. She still had the call detail saved on her phone. December the sixth, nine-twenty-one in the morning.

They told her to come as soon as she could. No, just come now, no appointment needed. That's when Lucy knew the news was bad. Doctors didn't rush you into the office to give you good news. They had a good laugh with you over the phone, *see, it was nothing to worry about*, and then they sent you on your way.

Lucy did not remember the drive to the doctor's office. She did not remember taking the forty-six steps from her car to the front door, she did not remember checking in, and she did not remember the additional thirty-eight steps to the doctor's private office. She sat alone on the couch for five minutes before the doctor joined her. The pediatrician sat next to Lucy on the couch, crossed one leg over the other. Her face looked grave.

"It's leukemia," said Dr. Webb.

Lucy simply stared at the doctor. She thought she should say something, but forming coherent words seemed like an impossible task right now.

She rocked back and forth in her seat, her hands clasped together on her lap.

"What kind?" Lucy finally whispered.

The doctor's shoulders sagged.

More bad news was coming. There were a few different types of childhood leukemia. The worst was acute myeloid leukemia.

"AML."

Lucy looked out the window at the parking lot. She could see her car, a five-year-old Subaru. They had taken their last normal ride in it. She had just paid it off, a feat of which she was quite proud. The car was hers and Emma's. They were beholden to no one.

She thought about all the things they had done together. Museums, hikes, trips to the beach. Last winter, they had tried snowboarding. Emma was a natural, loved it. They were planning to go between Christmas and New Year's. Emma was a bright and sweet girl, albeit sometimes a bit melancholy. Lucy attributed this to the absence of her father from her life. She had just started asking about Nate the Prick earlier that year. Try as she might, Emma could not understand why the other kids saw their daddies and she never did. He lived in Boston with his new wife and their twin boys. The coward. Easier to run off to another city and start over. She preferred not having to see him because she might break his nose if she did.

She considered telling Emma that her father was dead, but that seemed like a dangerous seed to plant.

Instead, she told Emma that some kids had one parent and some kids had two. That had bought Lucy some time, but it was only a temporary fix, a Band-Aid. And it certainly wasn't a perfect fix, because Emma continued to ask about him.

She chose not to tell Nate about Emma's illness. He didn't deserve to know anything about her. And if he wasn't willing to be part of her life when things were going well, what could they expect from him as they face the biggest challenge of her life? Was it cruel? Perhaps. But no crueler than the manner in which he had abandoned his young daughter.

"So where do we start?" asked Lucy, finally finding her voice.

"First step is induction," replied Dr. Webb. "Ten days of chemo, and then about a month, maybe six weeks of recovery. We'll see how she's doing, and then we'll move on to the second block of chemo, another ten days. After that, hopefully, she'll be in remission and we can move on to the second phase."

Lucy's head was spinning. Dr. Webb placed her hand over Lucy's and squeezed.

"I know this is scary," the physician said. "But we see very good results with this process."

"When do we start?" Lucy asked. She felt so helpless. All her years as a professional nurse, all her experience, all her knowledge, it seemed to evaporate under the heat of Emma's diagnosis.

The doctor's face turned to stone. All business now. A

fine line these doctors had to deal with. Empathy versus reality.

"Right away," she said. "Go get Emma, and she'll get her first injection this afternoon."

Lucy stood up, but her legs buckled. Dr. Webb caught her on her way down. She threw her arms around the pediatrician and began to cry. She stood in the office, holding onto this woman she barely knew for dear life, the room quiet but for the sounds of a desperate mother sobbing.

"LUCE?"

Manny startled her out of the horror show on a constant loop in her head. She didn't know what had brought it on. Perhaps it was the blank look on Tim's face.

"Sorry," she said.

She shook her head to clear out the fog and fuzz of days gone by. These flashbacks unnerved her, filled her with gloom for the rest of the day. As though she didn't have enough on her plate already. Her focus had to be on the here and now. Sitting here in this cafeteria had been a welcome salve from the wounds of the day. But as long as the lights were off, things would be different.

"Anyway," Tim was saying, "I was just telling Manny here that you're welcome to stay the night. I've got food and water and you can have a classroom that locks from the inside. It's not the Ritz Carlton, but it'll do in a pinch."

Lucy was touched by the offer, and she gave it serious thought. They were already here, they were safe, and they had provisions. Probably a lot more than thousands of others – perhaps even millions – had right now.

"Thanks, but we're fine," Manny said immediately.

"Hang on, Manny," she said. "We need to think about this. It's a couple more miles to Angela's. Things are probably worse than when we got here."

"Can I talk to you for a second?" Manny said, nodding toward the hallway.

"Okaaay," she said questioningly. Tim watched them with interest as they made their way through the crowd to the hallway. Irritation rippled through her. What was the man thinking? She wanted to throttle him right here in the cafeteria, if she was being honest. Tim was offering them safe harbor and Manny was jeopardizing it. Like a drowning man being offered a life preserver and asking for a minute to think it over. Although it was unnecessary, she pulled the door behind her hard, the loud slam echoing through the abandoned school to demonstrate her displeasure.

"What the hell's gotten into you?" she snapped. She tamped down her words in a harsh whisper, but they still boomed across the walls and down the darkened corridor. "This better not be because you want to party with your nursing school pals."

"No, Luce, of course not. It's him."

"The teacher? What about him?"

"Angela mentioned him to me once," he said. "He didn't take their breakup well."

"So? It happens. Maybe she broke his heart."

"Naw, he did some weird shit after."

"Like what?"

"Stalkerish kind of stuff. He'd follow her home. Kept showing up at her job. Sent her flowers all the time. She had to get a protective order."

Her stomach dropped.

Lucy pressed the heels of her hands against her forehead to stem the headache forming at her temples. Manny's words had given her serious pause, and she didn't know what to think. If Manny was telling the truth, then Tim could be dangerous. Obsessive exes who couldn't take no for an answer could unravel in an instant. And in the crucible of the current disaster, there was no way to know how he would react.

But that being said, Tim really didn't strike her as the type. It just didn't fit. Admittedly, she'd known the man less than an hour, and who was to say her instincts were serving her all that well right now?

She exhaled loudly.

"God, I just thought we'd caught a break here," she said.

"I know, Luce. Look, it's not far to Angela's. We'll be safe there."

"Manny, be honest. How much farther is it?"

"A couple miles. Three at the most."

Lucy did some calculations in her head. They had not

been making very good time, a mile every thirty minutes or so. At that rate, it would take close to two hours to make it to Angela's.

"What if they're not even there?"

"I've got a key."

"You do?"

"Yeah, sometimes they're still at work when I get up here."

She curled a lock of hair around a finger as she considered their predicament. Her gut was telling her something else, that Manny had this all wrong. She just didn't think Tim presented a threat to them. But she had verified intelligence in her hands. Manny wasn't one to exaggerate. Okay, he was, but he had specific details in this situation. A protective order! That meant a judge had decided Tim was enough of a threat to order him to stay away from Angela. She could not dismiss that out of hand.

Her gut was talking now.

If there was one thing she had learned as she approached her fortieth trip around the sun, it was never to ignore her gut. As a young nurse, she had interviewed for a job that she had really wanted in an intensive care unit at the University of Virginia Hospital. There were three interviewers, one about her age, one retiring, and the unit manager. They met in a conference room. The manager, Julia Thomas, sat at the far end of the long table while the other two sat close to Lucy.

It had struck her as odd, the woman struck her as

odd, and as the interview dragged on, a pit took up residence in Lucy's stomach. The interview did not go particularly well, perhaps because of Lucy's internal alarms sounding. When she walked out to her car, a wave of relief flowed through her. She felt like she'd dodged a bullet. She had never been so happy to blow an interview.

But then they had called her back for a second interview, this one with the Director of Nursing, and that had gone well. Lucy had ignored that feeling in the pit of her stomach, and she had accepted the job after all. And so began her gauntlet in the employ of Julia Thomas, as miserable a human being who had ever lived. She was a brilliant nurse who thrived on treating her charges like excrement. Turnover in the unit was high, but Lucy refused to quit, unwilling to let this woman dictate the course of her life. On a chilly October morning eighteen months later, Julia Thomas died in a motorcycle crash. At her funeral, Lucy thought about the day she had interviewed with her, and she recalled very strongly how she had ignored her gut.

And they were in a stressful situation. If Tim was prone to abnormal behavior when things were hunky-dory, then who knew what he was capable of when thrown into a crucible like the one they were now in. If he lost his cool, they would be in his blast radius. She couldn't afford that right now. Not with Norah to look after.

Damn.

"Okay," she said. "We'll keep moving. I think you've got this guy wrong, but I don't want to take any chances."

He flashed her twin thumbs up.

"It's the right call, Lucy."

"Let me do the talking."

Manny held up his hands in mock surrender.

"You got it, boss."

They made their way back to the lunch table, where Tim and Norah were playing rock-paper-scissors.

"Thank you for your hospitality," she said to him. "It was a real lifesaver. But I think we're gonna shove off. We don't want to be a burden, especially if you have people coming back here for shelter."

"Really, it's not a problem."

Lucy almost folded and accepted his offer, but she had to act on the hard evidence at hand. Evidence mattered.

"We'll be fine," she said. "But again, thanks so much for everything. It's been a rough day, and this was exactly the break we needed."

"It was my pleasure," he said.

An awkward silence fell over the group.

"And if it doesn't go your way at Angela's, my door will be open."

"Thanks," Manny said curtly. "We need to get going."

They accepted Tim's offer of additional supplies and loaded three abandoned backpacks with enough food and drink to last a couple of days. This was remarkably generous of him; Manny's intel about Tim left her wondering if he was deliberately indebting them to him in some way. Grooming her and Norah the way these devious predators did.

Tim escorted them to the emergency exit on the west side of the building. Before they set off, he gave them some rudimentary directions toward Angela's house. If there had been any doubt that Tim knew Angela, this information certainly took care of that.

"Be safe, guys," he said.

"You, too."

They lit the candle and continued westward. Lucy glanced back at Tim, who stood silhouetted by the candle he held in the school's open doorway.

Once again, they were on their own.

14

Manny stopped suddenly. Norah crashed into Manny's backside and tripped to the ground. Lucy, enveloped in a fog of exhaustion, stumbled over Norah's feet and nearly crashed to the sidewalk as well. She could not help but laugh the Keystone-Cops-ness of it all.

"This is it," Manny whispered.

They'd been walking for a while, long after time had stopped having any meaning. She had tried to keep track of time since they'd left Tim and the safety of the high school, but such a thing was impossible for the human brain. She didn't know why that was, but keeping track of something as elemental as time was beyond her capability. Could anyone accurately track the passage of a single minute?

Lucy's heart fluttered with relief.

The important thing was that it, regardless of whether

it had been thirty minutes or three hours, had been an uneventful sliver of time. They had moved in shadows and silence, avoiding other people; there were still clumps of people milling about, but no one paid them any mind. One moment, an angry dispute in the parking lot of an abandoned convenience store had left her heart in her throat. They had slithered by it unseen, and her pulse had been racing ever since. Several detours and retracings of their steps had extended their adventure even more than she had budgeted for this final stretch of the evening. She was dead on her feet. What a hell of a day it had been.

Norah had shuffled along quietly, staying close to Lucy, almost dependent on Lucy's movements rather than in control of her own. A dummy satellite. But the despair that had preceded her earlier flight seemed to have dissipated. Small favors. Crazy how a little food and drink could reset one's worldview.

"You sure?"

They were at the edge of a small shopping district; there was a residential neighborhood of small ranches and Cape Cods to the south. For all their fits and starts, their larks and frolics, Manny had gotten them here.

"Hell, yes. See that pizza place?"

She held up the candle, which had burned nearly down to the nub. In its flickering light, the restaurant's marquee was just visible. Ballston Pizza.

"It's delicious," he said. "Helps with the hangovers."

"What's a hangover?" asked Norah.

Lucy smiled. Kids always had their radar for adult themes perfectly calibrated. They could've talked recipes and politics for thirty minutes and Norah wouldn't have looked up, but you slide in a single reference to some adult-themed material, and kids were on that shit. Emma had been like that.

"Manny?" she said teasingly.

"Uh, a hangover?"

"Yeah, it's a funny word," Norah said.

"It is funny," Lucy said.

"So? What is it?"

"It's like a kind of flu that grownups can get," Manny said.

"How do you get it?" Norah asked.

"Overindulgence."

"What does that mean?"

"You'll have to look that one up," he said firmly.

Norah started to object, but Manny cut her off.

"Anyway, that place is awesome. And next door is a vape shop. Yeah, Luce! We're five minutes away!"

His voice was getting louder as he grew more animated. She shushed him.

"Yeah, sorry," he said. "I'm just so damn happy we made it."

"Good work, Manny."

She gave him a hug. He lifted her off the ground, obviously pleased with himself. Feeling renewed, the group picked up the pace, falling in behind Manny as he led them like the Pied Piper.

THE ROAD DESCENDED on a slight grade toward a long cul-de-sac, anchored by at least two dozen homes, Cape Cods and ranches. As they pressed down the road, Lucy detected activity ahead. The susurration of voices in the night air. The glow of fires burning. The squeal of children playing. The little neighborhood appeared to be in the midst of an impromptu street party. The road curled behind the shopping strip and into the neighborhood, which was guarded by a triangular-shaped copse of trees. Pine and maple. The trees served as an excellent natural barrier from the bustle of the busier commercial district behind them.

Lucy relaxed their pace a bit, planning their next move. The neighbors might be suspicious of interlopers. And if Angela wasn't home, then forget it. Even though Manny had a key, Lucy didn't think they'd be too keen on letting strangers just bowl on through and set up shop in the home of one of their own.

A pair of fire pits sat at the top of the road where it curled back away from the trees, down toward the score of homes arranged in a crescent surrounding the road's terminus. The flames danced in the night, the coronas rippling and crackling. In the immense darkness, there was something medieval about them. It reminded Lucy of castles and dungeons and knights and monks. It reminded her of danger.

A figure emerged from the shadows, silhouetted by

the fires blazing in the pits. He was a big fellow, as tall as Manny and sturdily built. He wore jeans and a t-shirt, and troublingly, he was holding a rifle in his hands. The fire pits were about fifty yards clear of the rest of the festivities. A perimeter of sorts. Already. Subtle hints of things to come. Ghost of Christmas Yet to Be.

"Need y'all to hold up," he said when they were about ten yards from one another.

Lucy signaled for her folks to stop.

"Can I help you?" asked the man.

His voice wasn't mean, but it wasn't exactly friendly either.

Lucy glanced at Manny and tilted her head, suggesting he take the lead here.

"Hey, man," Manny said, extending a hand and taking a step forward. "My name's Manny."

"How about you stay where you are?" the man asked, ignoring Manny's offer of goodwill. His grip on the rifle tightened. Lucy's heart skipped a beat. Again, she was regretting leaving Tim and the safe harbor of the high school.

"Just trying to be friendly, my man," Manny said, dropping his hand by his side.

"Okay," the man said. "What can I do for you?"

"My friends live here," he said. "Angela and Penny?"

"Congrats."

"We're here to see them."

"We're not letting folks in right now," he said. "Assume you're familiar with events currently unfolding."

"This is a public road," Lucy interrupted. "We have every right to be on it."

This seemed to catch the neighborhood sentinel off guard. Lucy sensed an opening, and so she moved in on it.

"Look, we're not here to cause trouble. Manny here went to nursing school with her."

"And you decided to pay a visit now?"

It was a good point.

"We were on a train that crashed today at Union Station," she said. "This girl lost her grandmother."

She placed her hand on Norah's head. She hated using Norah as a prop, but she had to exploit every advantage they had. And she would make it up to the girl. She would sit down with her when they had a free moment, and she would get to know her, give her the attention she deserved, that she was probably starving for.

The man's grip on the rifle loosened a bit, and the muzzle dipped toward the ground.

"Sorry to hear about your grandmother, sweetie."

"Thank you," Norah said in a small voice.

The man sighed.

"This is just beyond everything," he said. "I work at the National Archives. Took me six hours to get home. You'll have to forgive me. Things are a little wonky right now."

A woman joined them, emerging from the black void between the fire pits. She looked to be in her late fifties.

Her silvery hair was cropped close to her head. She wore .
khaki shorts and a sleeveless vest.

"What's going on?"

"You know Angela?" the guard asked. "The nurse?"

"Yeah," she said. "Sweet girl."

"Go tell her that her friend—"

He turned his attention back to Manny.

"Manny.".

"That her buddy, Manny, is here. With a woman and a
kid. And that they'd like to see her."

The bunker-like mentality of this neighborhood had
caught Lucy by surprise, which annoyed her. She was so
wrapped up in her own dilemma, in the story of Lucy,
that she had given little thought to what others might be
doing as the stars of their own movies.

First off, they were a bit of an anomaly, far from home
when the Pulse had hit. The vast majority of people
would have been close to home or, like Tim Whitaker, on
familiar ground. This put Lucy and her troupe at a severe
disadvantage. Neighbors would look out for one another.
Outsiders might be viewed as a threat. In a tightly knit
neighborhood, the effect would be even more dramatic.
This neighborhood struck her as the kind that lent itself
to tight bonds. Summer evenings at the pool, group
dinners, kids on the same soccer and baseball teams.
Cold bottles of beer clinked together while chicken and
burgers sizzled on the grill.

Lucy felt a pang of homesickness wash over her.
There, she would feel safe and secure. There, she could

handle whatever challenges this disaster would see fit to fling her way. She had loved the solitude and self-reliance that accompanied life on her little farm; moreover, in a situation like this, it would be a significant safety feature. Assuming Angela gave them refuge for the night, she thought it would be wise to shove off in the morning. If they could find bicycles, they could make it back to Richmond in a few days.

A shrill voice pierced through the darkness.

"Manny!"

Lucy craned her neck to locate the source of the voice. Coming up the street was a petite woman wearing blue nursing scrubs; her hair was pulled back in a ponytail.

Well, well, well.

The mysterious Angela.

Breaker of hearts.

Angela accelerated to a run and threw her arms around the much larger Manny. He embraced the smaller woman heartily, lifting her off the ground.

"It is so good to see you," he said.

"Can you believe this shit? What are you doing here? How did you get here?"

She talked very quickly, and that alone put Lucy off from her. Manny spent a couple of minutes recounting their day.

"Holy crap," Angela said after he finished recounting their tale.

"So, anyway, we were hoping we could stay here a

night or two. You know, until things settle down again and the power comes back on."

Manny was clearly expecting a quick yes, but things immediately became chilly. When Angela did not deliver a quick acquiescence, his face fell.

"You know, I would love to, but I'm not sure the neighborhood wants any overnight guests right now. Right, Derek?"

She was speaking to the sentinel who had intercepted them.

"Hey, it's your house. If you want to share your supplies, that's up to you."

"Great!" Manny said. "Two nights at the most."

Angela was holding up a single finger as if to slow Manny down.

"I'm gonna need to talk to Eric about this," Angela said. "We live together now."

"What about Penny?"

"She moved out. We had a bit of a falling out."

"Angela, it's me," Manny said. "I thought we were buds."

"Honey, we are. But I really need to talk to Eric about this."

He stepped toward Angela until their faces were inches apart. Lucy was standing two feet away; she could just make out what they were saying.

"Okay, you talk to Eric," Manny said.

"He's not here right now. He went to check things out."

"And remember to tell him about that favor you owe me."

Manny's voice had become tight and hard. Lucy had never heard him sound like that before. It was chilling.

"What are you talking about?"

Angela's voice had become equally tense.

"Oh, I think you know."

"Maybe you should leave," she said quietly.

Lucy became nervous; if Derek got the impression that they weren't welcome here, he might force them to leave.

"No, I don't think we will. I strongly suggest that you reconsider or you know what'll happen."

She laughed half-heartedly.

"You think they have time to deal with that right now? They've got too much on their plate."

He gestured grandly.

"This isn't going to last forever," he said. "And this is your chance to pay me back for what I did for you. Otherwise, I will be there with bells on."

Angela was quiet, her face awash with fright. Manny obviously held something very powerful over Angela's head. Now, it was Angela's turn for her face to fall and her shoulders to sag.

"Okay," she said, her head down, her eyes cut toward the ground. Manny reached out and squeezed her shoulder gently.

"We just really need your help," he said. "And after

this, we'll be even. You're like family to me. And family helps each other out. Right?"

The big tears that had welled up in her eyes reflected the flames blazing in the pit. She nodded. Manny smiled at Derek, who had been watching the proceedings with interest. Fortunately, he had been largely out of earshot, perhaps thinking it would have been rude to eavesdrop.

"They're gonna stay with us," she said to Derek.

Derek nodded.

Then she turned and disappeared back into the darkness.

"Are we good?" Lucy asked as they followed Angela down the street.

"We're good."

"So what's this favor she owes you?" Lucy asked, poking him in his side.

Manny did not immediately respond. He was ramrod straight, watching his friend recede into the darkness.

"I caught her diverting. Right before I moved to Richmond."

Lucy's heart fluttered. Manny had caught Angela stealing narcotics from the hospital where they'd worked. Narcotic diversion was one of nursing's cardinal sins. But a smart nurse knew how to exploit the system and could often get away with it undetected.

"And you covered for her," Lucy said.

Manny nodded.

"How did you catch her?"

"Wasting," Manny replied.

He did not elaborate. Typically, if a nurse withdrew more medication than the doctor had ordered for a patient, she was required to waste the excess in the presence of another staff nurse. But nurses in busy hospitals traded in trust and would often sign off on one another's waste without actually seeing what a coworker had disposed of. Nurses weren't supposed to do it, but things did get busy, and sometimes you couldn't find someone to witness. Manny must've seen her waste something that was not a narcotic. Or she had asked him to sign off without him actually witnessing it.

It begged a bigger question though.

"Why didn't you report her?"

And he should have. Failure to report such malfeasance was equally troubling. It may not have been as bad as the diversion itself, but it was a close cousin. Immediately, her respect for Manny had fallen a peg or two.

"She begged me not to," he said. "She said she wasn't using, and I believe her."

"Manny, that's what they all say."

"No, we worked together a lot. I never saw any signs of impairment."

"Some people are really good at hiding it. Doesn't mean she wasn't an addict."

"OK, listen, I'm pretty sure she was giving them to her boyfriend. He was selling it."

"Jesus, Manny. You're talking about six different felonies here."

"I know," he said. His voice was shaking.

A flash of understanding.

"It was this guy Eric, wasn't it?"

"Yeah."

Lucy scratched her forehead in disbelief. Eric, the man that Angela had left Tim for. Lucy was really second-guessing their decision to leave the high school. Granted, it was possible that everything Manny had said about Tim was true; perhaps Angela was attracted to bad boys. Troubled souls. After all, Tim could be both a high school teacher and a stalker. The two things were not mutually exclusive.

But Manny's revelation caused her to question everything she thought she knew about Angela. There were few things she detested more than nurses who broke the trust of the unit. Nurses had to work together to care for their patients; that was impossible without trust.

But all that aside, Manny had been right.

She did owe him a really big favor.

15

Lucy worried that Angela may change her mind, that the Pulse might convince her that his trump card held no power given the state of chaos. But she didn't seem keen on taking any chances. A valid report of diversion would likely end her career and possibly land in her jail. Manny might face repercussions as well for covering it up, but he was not likely to lose his license.

She led them through the gauntlet of fire pits down to the bottom of the cul-de-sac, where a party was indeed in full swing. They had set up grills and dragged out their coolers, heavy with ice, the cans and bottles of beer sweating in the May humidity. Ribbons of smoke curled from the line of grills, the air pregnant with the aroma of charred meats. Someone had set up a cornhole set; a match was underway. The weather had turned pleasant in the wake of the storm. In the clear skies, a full moon shone down on them.

Lucy couldn't decide if they were being optimistic or nihilistic. Certainly, they knew this was no ordinary blackout. She thought about how hard she, Norah, and Manny had fought for scraps, and that had only been the first afternoon. What if this dragged on for another week? Or longer?

She wanted to scream at them. They hadn't seen what she had seen. They hadn't seen planes fall from the sky. They weren't considering the worst-case scenario. But she was. She always did. Because for her, the worst of all worst-case scenarios had come to pass. Emma's leukemia was highly treatable, they had said. They had caught it early. Her odds of beating it were excellent. And she had let herself believe it. Because the alternative was too awful to contemplate. Even to the end, the bitter, heart-breaking, soul-shattering end, she had continued to believe that the odds were still in their favor.

But maybe they were considering the worst-case scenario. Maybe they knew that there would be difficult days ahead as they dealt with the fallout of today's catastrophic events. Because there would be extensive fallout even if the power came back on in the next five minutes. Maybe they were taking a little time to get their heads together before plunging into the work that lay ahead.

Then someone pressed a cold can of beer into her

hand, and she happily accepted it. Norah nipped at a can of soda. Lucy drank the beer down in two swallows; she could not remember a beer ever tasting quite so refreshing. It was like that first beer on a beach vacation still in its embryonic stages. The refrigerator was stocked, the cars unloaded, everyone sitting on the deck watching the waves lap at the beach as the sun dropped low behind you.

"Thank you for letting us stay," she said to Angela. "And cheers."

They clinked their beer cans together.

"Anything for Manny," she said.

She almost sounded sincere.

"So you work with Manny?"

"For three years."

"He's a good one," Angela said, glancing over at Manny. He had made friends with a couple two houses up from the center, undoubtedly regaling them with tales of the day's adventures. He was gesturing wildly with his arms, rotating his hands around each other as though to simulate their train car flipping over across the parking lot.

"Anyway, I promise we'll be out of your hair very soon."

"What if the power is still out?"

"I'm sure it will be back on by then. And if not, we can find some bicycles. Besides, I've got my own bed to sleep in. You're lucky that you're home for this. It's tough being this far from Richmond."

"Yeah," she said, reaching out and squeezing her arm. "I bet it is."

Actual sincerity that time.

As they traded pleasantries, Lucy picked up on a loud voice cutting through the revelry. The volume drew down the other noise from the party. At first, she couldn't make out the specifics, but then it hit her.

Eric.

"Angela!"

Angela's face paled in the moonlight.

"I think someone's looking for you," Lucy said.

"Yeah, that's my boyfriend," she said hesitantly, scanning the crowd for her man.

Lucy's jaw tightened. The other side of Angela's diversionary coin. Lucy tried to push it out of her head. This was not her problem, not now, not during this catastrophe. She would meet Eric, she would shake his hand and make nice. They would spend a little time getting their feet under them, and they would get the hell out of here. The crimes of Angela and Eric would have to be a story, a drama for another time.

"Eric!" she called out, waving her arms frantically.

A man slithering through the crowd stopped, attempting to triangulate the source of the voice calling him.

"I should go grab him," Angela said, her voice small and meek.

Lucy grabbed her by the elbow as she turned toward the crowd. She did not like the vibe she was getting; she began to wonder if Angela had participated in this diversion scheme voluntarily.

"Are you okay?"

"Fine," Angela said, her eyes glued on the crowd, waiting for Eric to emerge.

"Eric!" she called out again.

He finally spotted them and loped toward them like a panther on the hunt. He immediately made Lucy nervous. He was a big man. He wore jeans and a sleeveless black t-shirt, which exposed his massive arms. The shirt bore the logo of a heavy metal band called Burning Society. Lucy had been to one of their concerts on a first and only date with a radiologist from the hospital.

"Where the fuck were you?" he bellowed angrily.

"Sorry, honey," she said, wrapping her arms around him. He leaned down and gave her an open-mouth kiss, which Lucy thought was a bit over the top.

He noticed Lucy standing close by.

"Who's this?"

"This is Lucy," she said. "Remember my friend Manny?"

"Oh yeah, that faggot?"

Lucy cringed. Eric was coming in hard and fast, telling her everything she needed to know about him in less than thirty seconds. She appreciated his efficiency. An awkward silence followed.

"She and Manny work together in Richmond."

Eric eyed her closely, the old eye elevator, up and down. She expected it; men often leered at her. It was something she'd become used to over time. And it wasn't like she hadn't leered at a man before. Not nearly as often as they did, of course. Because they thought they were being so sly. To his credit, Eric didn't try to hide it. Normally, it didn't bother her, but coming from Eric, it felt sinister. This man was trouble. All of Lucy's sirens were blaring. A reminder that they were all on their own for now. There was no way to call for help. She would have to stay on her toes while they were here.

"How ya doin'?" he said, not really asking, more like to get the pleasantry out of the way.

"Good," she said, her brain on overdrive. It had been a mistake to leave the high school behind.

"The hell you all doing here?" he asked.

Angela cut in.

"Remember my friend Manny?" she said again.

Eric nodded his head slowly in a burst of understanding.

"Right. Manny," he said slowly, the words coated with contempt.

"So they're gonna stay with us for a couple of days."

"What?"

The news seemed to take him by surprise.

"Yeah," she said firmly. "Manny asked me for this favor."

Another head nod of understanding. He clearly didn't like what he was hearing, but he seemed to accept it.

"How long they staying?" he asked.

"Just a couple of days," she said. "Their train crashed, and they just need a little time to recover."

He sighed the annoyed sigh of a man who was used to getting his way. He would probably punish Angela for this later. He was a textbook abuser. It wasn't even his damn house, and he was acting like he owned it. But that was a problem for another day. Again, Lucy considered doubling back to the high school, but she discarded the idea just as quickly. Eric might worry that Manny would report Angela rather than cash in his favor. That would be good for no one, least of all Angela. Further, and more importantly, there was significant risk in making another journey through the deteriorating city at this hour.

Lucy wasn't sure if she liked Angela, but she did pity her. She had been with a man like Eric, briefly, getting out before things got too bad, so she understood Angela's dilemma. Men like Eric were a cancer; the longer you waited to treat it, the harder it became to extricate the malignancy from your life, and the greater the damage it inflicted. And she didn't want Angela to suffer if she could avoid it.

"A couple days," he said in a tone that suggested that his word was final.

Sunday couldn't get here soon enough. A couple of days would be all she could stomach in his presence. It was then she understood completely that Angela wasn't using the narcotic medication that she had diverted. Eric sold it. No question.

"Yeah, baby, I swear they're not staying long."

They couldn't get out of here fast enough.

THE STREET PARTY continued into the wee hours of the morning. Lucy ate two hot dogs and washed them down with two beers. Norah ate hugely, downing two hot dogs herself and two helpings of baked beans that someone had heated on the grill. Manny drank too much. But it was Eric that Lucy kept her eye on. He downed beer after beer, chain-smoking his way through two packs of cigarettes. He dominated every discussion he joined, never conceding a point. He talked about important people he had known, jobs he had done, always trying to paint himself as the power player in every scenario.

People seemed hesitant to call it a night. Doing so would be a concession that the fun was over, and with the power still out, no one wanted the fun to end. Because no one knew what would come after the fun stopped. But eventually, the party did wind down. There were hugs and long handshakes, an almost funereal tone to them. The crowd thinned slowly as people trickled home to get some rest and face down reality.

Norah, who had played hard after befriending a few neighborhood kids, had fallen asleep in a beach chair. Lucy gently shook her awake, careful not to startle her. What a day this girl had had. Lucy truly did not know what to do with her. Perhaps they needed to stay in town until Monday, until she could meet with someone in authority. She hated the idea of turning her over to Social Services, but there wasn't much choice. Dealing with abandoned kids was what Social Services was trained to do.

Norah slowly came to, and then she jumped in her seat as though she had forgotten where she was. She took a deep breath and let it out slowly. She looked around, the reminders of her current situation slowly sinking back in.

"Time for bed," she said.

She shook her head.

"Want me to carry you?"

Norah looked up at her with her wide, wet eyes. She nodded, and Lucy's heart broke. Just a kid. She had to make sure the kid was safe. That was all that mattered right now. Even if she didn't know what the parameters of that would entail.

She eased Norah out of her chair; the girl encircled Lucy's shoulders with her arms and wrapped her legs around her waist. She was as light as smoke. Norah nestled her head in the crook of Lucy's neck and fell asleep again. Lucy carried her up to Angela's house; Angela and Eric were sitting on the porch steps, sharing a joint.

"Ready to get some sleep?" Angela asked.

"She's tuckered out. Long day."

"Let's order some pizza!" bellowed Manny, stumbling down the walk toward them.

No one replied.

"Oh, right!" he said, giggling hysterically. "Can't!"

As Manny laughed at his own joke, Angela led them inside her bungalow, carrying a candle to light the way. The door opened onto a small family room ensconced in shadows. There was a sofa and loveseat positioned at a ninety-degree angle, oriented toward the large flat-screen television mounted on the wall. A stack of magazines sat on the coffee table, surrounded by empty boxes of takeout and fast-food bags. The air was redolent with the stench of cigarette smoke. Lucy did not smoke anymore, but she had while she was in the Army. The smell was repellent but familiar and comforting all the same.

"You all can sleep in here," she said, gesturing toward the room. "I'll get you some blankets and pillows."

Manny dropped his big frame on a recliner and fell asleep almost immediately. Angela returned with thin blankets and old pillows.

"Hey, I just want to thank you for letting us crash here," Lucy said. "It's just a real mess out there, and I'm not sure what we would've done without a safe place to stay tonight."

"It's nothing," Angela said tightly. "Good night."

"Good night," Lucy replied.

Angela disappeared down the hallway.

Manny was snoring. Norah stretched out on the sofa. Lucy sat next to her and gently eased her head into her lap. She barely remembered falling asleep.

16

L ucy woke with the sun streaming in through the east-facing window. As she had for each of the previous two mornings, she reached for her phone upon waking, praying the screen would light up, that the power had magically returned overnight. But still there was nothing. She stared at her blurry reflection in the glass inlaid into the dark void beyond, wondering what lay in store for them.

They were entering their second full day without power. As she lay on the couch, the massive quiet lingered. Absent was the hum of technology that had girded the foundation of their daily lives. But the sounds of nature were large. A bird was chirping, its rhythmic sing-song piercing the morning silence. Manny shifted in the recliner, muttering softly before rolling on his side and falling back asleep. Norah stirred but only just so.

She had underestimated the toll the crash would take. Once the adrenaline of the day had faded, the soreness had set in. She slept poorly that first night. Even the slightest movement triggered waves of pain in her core and back. The next morning, she could barely move. Every muscle hurt from head to toe. It even hurt to breathe. Manny didn't get out of the recliner until the sun started to set that evening. Norah had fared better, but even she was moving around gingerly like a little old lady. The day, which should have been spent on organization and planning, was lost to recovery. Any notion that they could begin the arduous journey back to Richmond that day quickly went up in smoke.

On the plus side, Angela had been a much more gracious host than Lucy had expected. She seemed to enjoy the company, enjoy having people around. Perhaps they were serving as a welcome buffer to the bone-on-bone experience that was life with Eric. That first day was quiet. Eric was gone much of the day; only God knew where. Angela told a few funny stories about Manny. They played Monopoly, a contest that had stretched well into the evening. Norah was quite the ruthless player. She snatched up properties quickly and, thanks to a few lucky rolls of the dice, grabbed the four railroads and several pricey monopolies, which she used to wipe out her opponents.

Just before dark, Eric returned after a long day rutting in the muck of their instant dystopia with tales to tell.

Lucy listened carefully as he spoke. Any intel about the wider world would be useful, even from an asshole like Eric.

"Made it all the way to the river," he said as they ate dinner by candlelight.

He and Angela ate Spam sandwiches. Lucy, Manny, and Norah, dined on pudding cups and apples sourced from the victuals Tim Whitaker had kindly sent them along with. She wondered how he was faring, how many kids were still under his watchful eye. By now, most of the parents and guardians would have retrieved their offspring. Most. Not all. Some kids would be like Norah. Orphaned or stranded. At least those kids were close to home, not drifting along with strangers in a faraway land.

"A lot of fires burning," Eric went on. "Did hear some gunfire."

"Food and water?" Lucy asked.

"Gone. I stopped at a few markets. Absolutely cleaned out."

"What about crowds? A lot of people out?"

"Some," he said. "Not many. Maybe folks looking for trouble. Came across a National Guard unit telling people to go home."

People like you, Lucy thought.

"What are we gonna do?" Angela said. "Our food isn't gonna last forever."

Eric didn't reply; he scratched his two-day-old stubble as he stared into the candle's flickering corona.

"Eric?" Angela said.

"Don't worry about it," he said. "I'll take care of it."

After dinner, they worked on a puzzle that Angela had found in the bedroom; working by candlelight was difficult and they gave up after an hour. Norah was sleepy, and Lucy herself had a hard time focusing on anything. Lucy tucked Norah in on the couch. Manny and Eric sat on the porch drinking and smoking cigarettes.

"What are we gonna do tomorrow?" Norah asked sleepily.

"I want us to rest one more day and then we'll leave. How does that sound?"

"Good."

Lucy brushed the girl's hair from her face.

"Can I tell you something?" Norah asked

"Sure."

She sat up and looked around.

"I don't like it here," she whispered.

Lucy smiled wanly in the darkness. She didn't like it here either.

"We'll be gone before you know it."

"Okay."

While the men sat out front, Lucy made her way to the backyard and stretched out on an old wooden Adirondack chair. The sky was clear and moonless, rippling with starlight. Absent the light pollution, the universe could show her wares as they were meant to be seen. It was quite beautiful. Lucy desperately wanted the power to come back on, but the beauty of the natural sky was undeniable.

Lucy slept better the second night. As her muscles healed, the ibuprofen was doing a better job shutting down the pain. Lucy held back a chuckle when Angela said she wished she had something stronger to offer her. She didn't doubt that Eric and Angela kept a stockpile somewhere in the house. To be fair, purloined pills might prove useful as currency in the coming days. Undoubtedly, Eric had already considered that.

Lucy got up and used the bathroom. As she washed her hands, she studied her face in the mirror. There was some bruising along her left cheekbone. She pulled up her shirt and palpated her left flank, which was still sore, almost seventy-two hours after the accident. More bruising along her left hip. The pain was centered in her lower back now. It felt like someone had used a vise on the muscles running up and down her spine. The good news was that her headache was fading. She dry-swallowed two ibuprofen tablets from Angela's medicine cabinet. She quietly poked around the cabinet, looking for narcotics, finding none.

Lucy doubted that Angela and Eric had abandoned their diversion scheme since Manny's departure. There was too much money at stake, especially if they had a reliable fence that could move the product for them. A single pill could fetch ten bucks on the street. And as long as she was smart about it, never taking too much, always closing the documentation loop, never showing up on the unit's audit reports, there was really no way to catch her.

The bathroom was unremarkable. A hand towel embroidered with American flags hung from the towel rack ring mounted next to the sink. An air freshener sat atop the toilet tank, infusing the air with a hint of cinnamon. So ordinary. She loved the ordinary, she loved the routine. Routine was her jam. A good book. A bingeworthy show. A cup of hot tea. Her jammies. Especially after a long day at the hospital.

Twelve-hour shifts were often nothing but straight chaos. Hers was an urban hospital smack in the middle of the city that included a large college campus, dangerous neighborhoods, and multiple assisted living facilities and nursing homes. There was no routine, there was no ordinary at work. On any given day, she might help treat a child with a gunshot wound in her stomach and a great-grandmother with bedsores so bad that she had stuck to her bed sheets. And that was during normal circumstances. The coronavirus pandemic had been particularly rough on healthcare workers. Lucy herself had come down with the virus; she was one of the lucky ones and was back on her feet after a week. The virus had cut a terrible scar into the world, it was barely behind them, and already they were facing something just as bad.

And Emma's illness? More chaos. It was easy to believe that there was a routine to the treatments, the doctors' appointments, and the side effects of the chemotherapy. But it was chaos to its very core simply dressed up to look like routine. Chaos in disguise, concealing the roiling, agonizing misery. They expected her to remain calm, to act like it was routine, to act like it was normal to have to take your child to these terrible appointments, any one of which could end with the passing of a death sentence.

What she wouldn't give for a little ordinary right now. That's why home was so important to Lucy. A good meal. A good sleep. A few chapters of a book. Maybe a run. Ordinary. She lived her life in routine now because it protected her sanity. As she poked through Angela's bathroom knick-knacks, a wave of profound sadness washed over her. It felt like things wouldn't be ordinary and routine again for a while.

When she returned to the living room, Norah was awake and flipping through a magazine. She snuggled underneath her blanket and looked as relaxed as Lucy had seen yet. Manny was awake but nowhere to be found.

"Hey," she said. "Did you sleep okay?"

Norah nodded, stifling a yawn as she did so.

She was really a striking young girl. Her jet black hair framed her perfect face, long and angular. Her skin was extremely dark, almost like she was constantly in silhouette. Her eyes were a deep brown, flecked with gold and highlighting her high cheekbones. The type of good looks that would both help and hurt down the road. And it would only worsen as she got older and men began paying attention to her. A desire to keep Norah safe throbbed deeply inside her.

Emma would have been around the same age as Norah was now. God, she missed that kid. Here it came, a surprise bombing run of grief, strafing her soul until she could no longer stand it and it left her wrecked and weak and sometimes just curled up in a ball on her bed. If it hit her at work, she could usually lock it away until the end of her shift. But sometimes, she couldn't, and her coworkers would cover for her while she took a ten-minute break in her car, sobbing hysterically, cursing at a God she did not believe in, pounding the steering column so hard that sometimes she'd worry she'd broken a bone in her hand.

The day lay before them like an open book. It was shaping up to be a hot one, already well into the eighties; even with the windows open, the house had warmed up quickly. Lucy would spend the day planning their departure; they would leave the following morning, at first light. She checked their remaining supplies, laying them all out on the coffee table. Three cups of applesauce, two puddings, and six granola bars. Water wasn't an issue yet. Virtually all municipal water systems relied on gravity to deliver water from the reservoirs, even in buildings up to seven stories tall. But without power to refill them, those reservoirs would empty quickly, especially in light of the massive demand. She would suggest they start filling cups and bottles and bathtubs.

The situation was not ideal.

As Lucy repacked their supplies into the backpack, Angela joined them in the living room. She was drinking a Diet Coke and looked exhausted. Dark circles fluttered underneath her eyes, which were quite red.

"We're gonna shove off in the morning," Lucy said immediately. She wanted to get ahead of overstaying their welcome. Putting a concrete expiration date on their visit would be a good way to do that, put her mind at ease, and keep Eric off their backs.

Eric himself was nowhere to be found that morning, and Lucy hoped that he had left already. Maybe they'd gotten lucky and the couple had broken up during the night.

"Okay," Angela said disinterestedly. She didn't seem to care.

Bad news arrived a few minutes later. Eric stomped into the living room with a cigarette dangling from the corner of his mouth. He wore cargo shorts and no shirt, exposing his massive chest and arms. A Confederate flag was tattooed just above his right nipple. He was a big and angry man, and there were few things that Lucy feared more.

"You make some breakfast, Ang?"

"Not yet," she said. Her face was pale.

He started barking at her for this indiscretion, but she cut him off.

"Just wanted to be sure what you wanted, baby," she said.

"Go make me a sandwich," he snapped. "And grab me a beer."

As Angela made her way to the kitchen, he plopped

down on the recliner and lit another cigarette. He pulled the bill of his baseball cap down over his bloodshot eyes.

"What the fuck's wrong with the power?" he snapped.

"I think it was an EMP," Lucy said.

"An EM-what?"

She gave him the brief summary she had shared with Manny. Then he asked a question that she hadn't considered.

"How come all the cars are dead? A lot of them don't have electronics."

That was beyond her level of expertise.

"It's a good question," she said. "I don't know. Maybe some are still working."

"Christ," he muttered.

The air clouded with cigarette smoke.

"You mind not smoking inside?" asked Lucy as sweetly as she could. She even leaned forward to show a little cleavage. "It's bad for little lungs."

Lucy subtly tilted her head toward Norah as though to suggest she and Eric were co-conspirators, on the same side, both thinking about the best interest of the child.

"Yeah, I fuckin' mind," he said, not even looking up. He followed up his refusal with a trio of smoke rings.

She took a deep breath and let it out slowly. The man was straight trash.

Angela returned from the kitchen with a peanut butter sandwich and a lukewarm beer for her man. He ate quietly, indifferent to Angela's houseguests.

"I'd offer you something," she said, "but we really don't have much."

Lucy waved her off.

"We're fine."

She considered telling Angela about her old boyfriend Tim's altruism, but it probably wouldn't have gone over well with Eric. Angela had clearly fed Manny a load of bullshit about Tim. She wondered if Tim had also known about Angela's diversion. She had probably stolen drugs at the school; it would have been much easier to do it there, as the internal controls on the medications were not likely to be as robust as in a hospital setting. It might have given Eric and Angela motive to smear Tim's name. Or at least motive to threaten to do so.

"Again, sorry."

Lucy waved her off.

The cul-de-sac was abuzz with activity, the sounds of life filtering in through the open windows. People came and went from house to house, desperate to share or learn the latest bit of gossip that had filtered its way into the neighborhood. A few brave souls ventured out but returned within a couple of hours with nothing new to report.

The front door swung open, triggering quite a response from Eric. He tossed his plate onto the coffee table and drew a gun, which had been concealed in the waistband of his shorts

It was Manny. His mouth widened into a shocked *O* when he saw the gun pointed at him.

"It's just me!"

"How about you knock next time?" said Eric, sliding the gun back into his shorts.

To Lucy's disappointment, he did not accidentally shoot himself in the balls.

"Where you been, Manny?" asked Eric.

"Talking to the neighbors," he said. "People are getting worried. Like it's the end of the dang world."

Panic was setting in. Not the high-octane stuff. Low-grade. A pot of water slowly coming to a boil.

"How can everything be out like this?" asked Angela, a hint of panic spicing her voice.

"Shut up, Ang," Eric snapped.

He got out of his chair.

"How much food we got left?"

"Few days," Angela replied.

"Let's count it up."

It was a good idea, Lucy had to admit.

"We'll help," she said.

They set up shop in the kitchen. Angela sat at the table with a pen and a pad of paper. Eric acted as the project manager. Unfortunately, the cupboard was mostly barren. Nurses were young and busy and preferred going out to staying home and cooking; at least that had been her experience. Eric withdrew the few canned goods from the pantry one by one.

Angela dutifully recorded the inventory on the legal pad.

Two cans of black beans.

One can of Spam.

Three cans of diced tomatoes.

Two jars of spaghetti sauce.

Four cans of tuna.

One box of Honey Nut Cheerios.

Eric dug into the box and pulled out a scoop.

"Stale," he said with a mouthful of cereal.

One box of spaghetti and one box of penne pasta.

"And there's nothing in the fridge?" asked Eric.

"Not really," Angela said timidly.

She opened the fridge door. It was barren but for a few beers, a few cans of hard seltzer water, and bottles of condiments and salad dressings. There were some carrots and apples in the produce drawer. She and Eric had finished the other perishables in the fridge the day before. There wasn't much.

Eric began making strange sounds with his tongue as though he were deep in thought. To the extent he was capable of such thought. Christ, she really needed to stop this and make an ally of this man at least until the morning.

He slammed the door. It made a thick whooshing sound as it closed. Eric was deprived the satisfaction of a good door slam, which seemed to irritate him even more.

"Need to make a supply run," Eric announced.

He pointed at Manny.

"You're coming with me."

"I am?"

"Yeah," he said. "Need another set of eyes out there."

"Where you going?" asked Lucy. "You said the stores are cleaned out."

"I have a plan."

"I'll go too then," Lucy said.

"You'll just slow me down," Eric said.

Lucy bristled with annoyance. She could kick both men's asses six ways to Sunday, but Eric had picked Manny because he was a man. She stifled a sigh. It got tiresome. No matter how used to it she was.

"I was in the Army, you know," she said testily.

"You see combat?" Eric snapped back.

"Yeah. Have you?"

This shut him up and probably embarrassed him. As good as it made her feel, she regretted the dig.

"We'll have each other's backs out there," she said, looking for détente. "Six eyes are better than four. Trust me, man, I know. Plus, it's an extra set of arms to carry supplies. We may only get one chance at this. We need to get as much as we can today. Right now."

Eric scraped the stubble on his square chin as he considered it.

"You better know what you're doing out there."

"I can take care of myself," Lucy said.

He hemmed and hawed.

"Look, it was rough out there yesterday, right?"

He nodded.

"It'll be worse today. People are gonna start panicking. Three's a crowd, and I mean that in a good way. People will leave us alone."

"Fine."

"And we split whatever we find," Lucy said, bracing herself for an explosion. "Fifty-fifty."

"No," Eric said. "You get a third."

Lucy shook her head.

"There's three of us," she said. "And two of you. And we have a long trip ahead of us tomorrow. Half."

She considered reminding Angela of her obligation to Manny, but she held her tongue. That would likely blow up in her face.

"Fine," he said.

"You okay watching after Norah?" Lucy said to Angela.

Angela nodded, smiling broadly. She was probably relishing the idea of a few hours with Eric out of her hair. Norah probably made for far better company.

"We'll be fine," Angela said. "We'll keep working on that puzzle."

They spent the next forty-five minutes outfitting themselves for the upcoming journey. As she predicted, the water was still running just fine. They filled up water bottles. She left the snacks, wanting to make sure Norah had something to eat.

"There is something y'all should work on," Lucy said.

"Name it," Angela replied.

"Fill up bottles, cups, and pots and pans with water."

Angela nodded.

Lucy ruminated a moment longer.

"How many bathtubs you got?" she asked,

"Two."

"Fill them both. That will give you a few days' supply. Nothing more important than water."

"Good idea," Eric said.

"You have any other pieces lying around?" Lucy asked. "I'm a pretty good shot."

"Nope."

"You sure? It could be rough out there. You'll appreciate having some backup if things get nasty."

He didn't reply, but his eyes glittered at the possibility of urban combat. She suspected that would excite him. Men like Eric drove her insane. Never satisfied with peace and quiet. Always thinking they were destined for greatness forged in fire and blood. Functions of unfulfilled lives.

"Honestly, if I had another one, I'd give it to you."

No doubt that he was lying. Probably wanted to maintain control of their group.

"How about a knife? I'm pretty good with that too."

"Yeah, there's one in the bedroom."

He disappeared down the hallway to retrieve it. As they waited for him to return, Lucy took Norah aside. The girl was anxious at the prospect of being left alone with Angela. Which was to be expected. But she needed to go with Manny and Eric. She did not trust Eric to get the job done correctly. And they needed to earn their keep for the rest of the day.

"Don't go," Norah said in a small voice.

"I'm won't be gone long," Lucy said. "But we need to find some food. You still want to leave tomorrow, right?"

"Yeah."

"Then we need to do this."

"Can I help too?"

Lucy lay a gentle hand on the side of Norah's face. A strong urge to keep this child safe washed over her again. It had been a long time since she had felt a connection with someone. Just a human connection, free of motive or agenda.

"I'm sure Miss Angela would love for you to help out with filling up the water bottles," she said. "We want to thank her for letting us stay here for so long."

She glanced up at Angela.

"Can we do another campfire tonight?" asked Norah.

Lucy smiled. At least the novelty of the situation was still fresh for someone. For kids, it probably was exciting. A break from the routine, the ordinary. And maybe it was like that for other people. The kind of thing that made you sit up and take notice of your life. Figure out what was really important. But Lucy had already been through that. Circumstances dictated that you abandon all non-essential functions in favor of the things that were the most important.

Like this little girl.

"Of course," Lucy said with as much verve as she could muster. The longer Norah looked at this as an adventure, the better. Important to keep her calm.

"We'll be back soon, okay?"

Norah nodded and then threw herself against Lucy, hugging her tightly. Lucy hugged her back, feeling tears bubble to the surface.

"It's gonna be okay."

Angela and Norah watched from the porch as they set out. As the trio eased into the curve around the copse of trees, Lucy turned back and waved at Norah.

She waved back.

17

The sun was directly overhead. The day had broken hot and clear, the sky a deep blue on this late spring afternoon. It was quiet as they followed the road back out to the main drag, passing the two fire pits guarding the neighborhood. The blackened remains of last night's blazes sat cold. Each of them carried a bundle of plastic shopping bags. For some reason, Lucy felt a little guilty about her intent to use plastic bags. On the other hand, the fact that no cars were running likely made up for this carbon footprint. Either way, the environment would have to wait.

"So what's this plan?" Lucy asked.

"There's a food distribution warehouse about a few miles from here," Eric said. "I was a truck driver back in the day, used to run loads outta there."

"Are you still a truck driver?"

"No."

"What do you do now?" Lucy asked.

She was genuinely curious about what this man did to support himself.

"I work for myself," he said cryptically.

Lucy choked down a chuckle. He might as well have said that he worked in waste management. She pictured the path of those purloined opioids, burrowing their way into the lives of those they would soon destroy. Opioids were a scourge. Worse than guns.

"Anyway, that warehouse feeds into a bunch of the grocery stores around here. And most people don't know about it."

He was right. Most folks would think to go right to their local market; people rarely stopped to consider the other links in the supply chain. A well-stocked distribution center could be a gold mine. She made a mental note to figure out where the closest one to home was.

"We just gonna steal this stuff?" Manny asked.

"You got a better idea?" Eric asked.

"Eric's right," Lucy said through gritted teeth. She squeezed Manny gently on the elbow.

"This is definitely the smart move."

She turned her attention back to Eric.

"How long until we get there?"

"An hour," Eric replied. "It's on the north side of town."

They reached the shopping strip at the intersection. Lucy's shirt was damp with sweat, clinging to the small of her back. It was quiet here. A man and a woman crossing the street away from them disappeared into a small neighborhood across the way. Other than that, there was very little activity. It had been about seventy-two hours since the Pulse. The world's natural momentum would keep civilization civilized for a little while. Eventually, though, that would change. People would run out of food and medicine and water, and then the next phase in this new paradigm would begin.

But for now, it was quiet. People hunkering down, sheltering in place, or out hunting for supplies. Hoping for the best. Hoping the power would come back on. There would be looters, of course, because there were always looters. Would they know to loot the right loot?

How much loot could a looter loot if a looter could loot loot?

"We're gonna head north here," he said.

"That's where the commercial and industrial areas are?"

He nodded.

They continued on that heading for a while. A while, a while, a while. There was no way to know how long a while. Fifteen minutes? Thirty minutes? Seventeen seconds? How much they had relied on these discrete blocks of existence. Seconds, minutes, hours, days, weeks, months, years. What did *a while* even mean? It could mean anything.

Emma.

Lucy had her only a short *while*. She was sick only a little *while*. Who decided what a while was? Because it sure seemed like a damn eternity to Lucy when she was sick. And then when she was gone, it didn't seem like a very long time at all.

They had made their machines their gods. All of them subservient to machines to tell them something as simple as the time with any sort of accuracy. It was a reminder how much they had relied on their machines. Once again, she willed the power to return, so it could save them from themselves. Save them from their own shortsightedness, from their own incompetence.

"Y'all know this was an attack, right?" Eric said over his shoulder. "The towelheads or maybe the Chinese did this. They're gonna come in now, try and take over."

He chuckled softly.

"Like to see them try."

He appeared to be having a conversation with himself.

"You might be right," she said.

Eric's racism-infused belief that this had been an act of war was an interesting one. She hated agreeing with him, but it also built a reservoir of goodwill with him that she might have to withdraw from later. And it was certainly possible. If you could neuter your opponent's ability to launch a counterstrike, the battle was already won.

As she considered this, she noticed a discordant sound somewhere in the distance. It sounded like someone yelling.

"Hey, hold up a second," she said, her ears working to triangulate the location of the sound.

The others paused.

"You guys hear that?"

"No."

"Like someone shouting?"

Eric's face tightened with concentration; Manny tilted his head skyward and scrunched up his face as they tried to dial in to her frequency. Lucy picked up on the sound again a few seconds later. A flash of understanding bloomed across the men's faces.

"Yeah, what of it?" asked Eric.

"Someone's in trouble."

"The fuck do I care? Lotta folks in trouble right now. Including us, I might add."

Angry heat flashed through her body like lightning. He was such a miserable asshole.

"Maybe it's someone we can help," she said.

"Don't care," he said. "We've got our own shit to deal with."

"No, dammit, we are going to see if we can help."

"Fuck that."

"You do what you want. I'm going."

He huffed loudly.

"Look," she said. "I know a lot of people are in trouble. But listen to that."

Right on cue, another stitch of wailing.

"We could help someone right now," she said. "I won't ask again."

She could see him working it out. He seemed to understand that he needed their help. And that was their trump card. He could only carry so much by himself, and worse, he couldn't protect himself from bandits. So she would use that to her advantage.

"Wait here," she said. "I'll see which direction it's coming from. If you can still hear it, give me a thumbs up."

She continued south fifty yards, but the already muted wails faded away entirely. She looked back at the men; Manny was flashing a thumbs up. She backtracked to her starting point and recalibrated. The mournful wailing picked up again. Someone was calling for help, literally the word "help" that had degraded into part howl. She went west this time, but that also proved to be a dead end.

Back to the starting point.

On to the third point of the compass rose.

As she trekked eastward toward a gas station parking lot, the cries grew more intense. She froze in between two pump islands, where six vehicles sat abandoned. Two still had the pump nozzles inserted in their gas tanks. She crossed the tarmac and edged up to the doors. The windows and doors had been shattered, bits of safety glass littering the sidewalk like puddles. The place was completely picked over, the shelves bare.

"Heeelllllppp," came the cry.

She went inside, confused. Why would anyone be here? Maybe they were injured, incapacitated in some way. It could be a trap, although it wouldn't be a very good trap. There were a million better ways to scam someone. A faint banging sound came from somewhere in the back. She ventured a little deeper into the store and called out.

"Hello? Is someone here?"

"Yes!" came a reply, followed by sobs. "I'm in the closet!"

The voice had a sharp Indian accent, female.

Lucy zig-zagged through the empty aisles to the back of the store. A door marked *EMPLOYEES ONLY* caught her eye. Someone had wedged a small stepladder under the stainless steel door handle, which had made it impossible to open from the inside. She hustled up to the door, kicked the stepladder aside, and pulled the door open. A petite woman tumbled out into Lucy's arms, barely able to hold herself up. Lucy wasn't prepared for the sudden embrace, and the women toppled to the ground. Lucy climbed back to her feet, but the woman remained on the ground, apparently too weak to stand up. A horrific stench emanated from the small closet.

The woman began to sob, her entire body spasming. Lucy knelt down and helped the woman up to a seated position. It was too dark to see her face, but she was rail thin, barely five feet tall. She smelled terrible, a rich mixture of decay and body odor and human waste. Lucy fought the urge to gag, but a dry heave got away from her. The woman did not seem to notice. Luckily, it was too dark to see inside the closet. They sat in the gloom as the woman collected herself.

"They left me," she said in between desperate gulps of air. "They left me. They left me."

She sagged against Lucy and buried her head into her shoulder.

"They left me."

"It's okay," Lucy said to her, holding the woman close and breathing through her mouth.

It wasn't hard to figure out what had happened. Looters had locked her in the closet while ransacking her store. She might have been in here for as long as three days. Three days without food and water, alone in the closet. There wasn't even enough room to sit down, let alone lie down. If she had slept, she'd had to do it standing up. It was probably eighty-five degrees in the store, even hotter in the closet. It must have been hell on earth.

"They left me," she said again.

"Let's get you outside," she said.

"Manny!" she yelled out. "Get in here!"

"Coming!"

Manny appeared out of the gloom.

"Help me get her up."

They each took an arm and lifted the clerk off the ground. She was delirious, barely aware of her surroundings. She repeated the phrase – *they left me* – over and over as they eased their way outside. At the threshold, the woman began to shriek; she threw her hands over her eyes like a vampire as they stepped into the sunlight. After so much time in darkness, her wide-open pupils were torched by the sunlight.

"It's okay," Lucy reassured the woman. "Let's sit down."

Eric and Manny stood awkwardly under the shade of the gas pump as the woman continued to weep.

"Get me some water."

Eric hesitated.

"Now, dammit!"

Eric handed her a bottle from his pack. She offered it to the woman, who did not accept it. She was badly dehydrated, so Lucy held the bottle to her lips and tilted the bottle upward. A splash wet the woman's lips, but she did not open her mouth to accept more. A few ounces splashed onto the concrete.

"Don't fucking spill it," Eric barked.

"What's your name?" asked Lucy, ignoring him.

The woman's name – Akhila – was printed on the name tag pinned above her filthy red polo shirt. But Lucy wanted to connect with her on a personal level, and this seemed as good an entry point as any.

"They left me," she repeated.

"I know," Lucy said. "But they're gone. You're safe."

"They left me. They left me."

A braid of worry wormed its way through Lucy. Akhila's eyes were glassy, and there was a spacey, faraway look on her face. It was difficult to determine what effect her time in the *de facto* deprivation tank had had on her.

"We ain't got time for this," Eric said. "It'll be dark before long and I want to be home before then."

"Just give me a minute," she said. "Let's get her back to reality. I'm not sure she knows where she is."

Lucy sat quietly with Akhila on the curb, holding the woman's hand and patting it gently. She wanted the woman to know that she was safe, that she was free. It was possible Akhila hadn't even realized that she was outside yet. That kind of sensory deprivation could wreak havoc on someone within a few hours, and she'd been subject to it far longer than that. She might have believed that she was hallucinating, that she was still in the closet. Part of her might always wonder whether she was still in the closet. That was what trauma did to you.

She offered Akhila the bottle a second time, and again, the woman pushed it away. Lucy gave up; when the woman got thirsty, she would drink. Lucy screwed the cap back on the bottle and set it on the curb.

"How about this?" Eric asked. "We leave her here with a bottle of water and a granola bar. She can have a snack whenever she's ready and then she can mosey on home."

The idea of leaving this woman here by herself curdled Lucy's stomach. But she didn't know what else she could do for her. She was safe; they would leave her with a little water and food. Probably more than many people had right now. They would move her into the shade of the overhang, where she would be safe from the sun's rays. Also, it would be difficult to spot her from the street, keeping her safe from bandits.

"Okay, help me move her into the shade."

Eric almost acted magnanimously about it. He knelt down and gently drew Akhila's arm around his shoulder. Then he and Lucy rose to their feet, lifting the petite woman with them. She was dead weight, but she was not heavy; it was like carrying a small bundle of branches.

As they turned, Akhila's bare foot caught the edge of the curb. And that was when everything went straight to hell. She squealed in pain, violently twisting and turning, attempting to break free of Lucy's and Eric's grip.

Her sudden burst of activity took them by surprise. Eric stumbled backwards and down onto his seat; Lucy tripped forward, landing on her hands and knees. She winced as her knees scraped against concrete and broken glass. As she climbed to her feet, a heavy weight crashed down on her back, flattening her to the ground.

Akhila was screeching and pounding her fists into the back of Lucy's head. Lucy barely had time to cover her head with her hands, stunned by the virulence of the woman's attack. Lucy was heavier than the woman, and she worked that to her advantage. As Akhila rained down blows on Lucy's back, she steadied her legs under her. Akhila had now wrapped the crook of her elbow under Lucy's chin; her forearm slipped under Lucy's jaw and crimped her windpipe. From the corner of her eye, Lucy spotted Manny staring dumbfounded at the scene unfolding before him.

It felt like it had been going on for an hour, but the attack had only been underway for a few seconds. As she struggled to hang on to her consciousness, Lucy came up with a plan. Akhila was now riding her like a horse and holding on for dear life. Lucy rotated her position, preparing to drive Akhila backwards into the wall to shake her loose. Her airway had narrowed significantly, and her body screamed for oxygen. Her head felt swimmy.

As Lucy pivoted, Eric climbed back to his feet and stepped toward the melee. He peeled Akhila from Lucy's back like she was a Band-Aid and threw her to the ground. Lucy gasped with relief, gulping down huge, sweet gobs of air. The swimminess dissipated.

The next few seconds unfolded like a time-lapse video. Eric drew his gun and pointed it down at the woman, who had pushed herself up on her hands and knees.

"No!" shrieked Lucy.

But Eric ignored her. He fired a bullet into the back of the woman's head. Blood, bone, and brain matter splattered the sidewalk. The report of the gunshot echoed loudly, making it feel like Lucy had cotton stuffed in her ears. Akhila's lifeless body tumbled facedown to the sidewalk like a sack of groceries.

Lucy stared at the dead woman, stunned at the spasm of violence, wondering how it had gone so badly so quickly. Eric had executed this woman in cold blood, and she had no idea what to do now.

"Why?"

The only word that Lucy was able to eke out.

"She was a threat," Eric replied. "Had to put her down."

He spoke as though this were no big deal. But he was trembling.

A grim realization pierced Lucy's soul. Nothing would happen to Eric for killing this woman. They couldn't call the police. No ambulance would come. This woman would lie here dead and her body would begin to rot. No one had come looking for her. Perhaps she had no friends, no family, no one wondering where she was. Perhaps her people had already been lost to this catastrophe. And when it was all over, and they had moved to the new status quo, there would be no justice for Akhila. Just another statistic.

"You didn't have to do that," Lucy said.

"The fuck I didn't. She was insane. She might've killed you."

"But you had gotten her off of me. She was just scared, confused. That was totally unnecessary. That's not how we do things."

Manny's face had blanched. He was still staring at the woman's body. Lucy didn't know if Manny had ever seen such an act of extreme violence. He certainly had seen the aftermath in the emergency department, but that was much more clinical. This was straight in-your-face horror. Lucy had become familiar with this kind of horror while serving overseas. But Manny hadn't. Most people hadn't. The good people in the affected area were about to get a very graphic education.

And even though she had been down this road before, it didn't make it any easier to witness. No one needed to see what she had seen. It didn't make her better, stronger, smarter. Horrible things were just that. Horrible. There was no lesson to be learned. And for better or worse, they had all lived in a soft society. There was nothing wrong with that. Humanity had worked hard to make life not so hard. That was the whole point. Eating Chinese takeout on her couch with her dog was a hell of a lot better than hunting for her next meal.

For that reason, they desperately needed the power to come back on. They were barely seventy-two hours into this crisis and already civilization was eroding. She could only imagine the horrors that already had been wrought. Society wasn't ready for this.

"We are not going to do this," Lucy said. "Do you understand me?"

"I'll do what it takes to stay alive," he said. "I suggest you think about doing the same."

He drifted over to the far edge of the parking lot; he lit a cigarette and faced the sun beating down on them. Lucy watched him smoke and hated him. She hated him for being right. Because if the power didn't come back on soon, if this was more widespread than she already feared, then Eric would be right. His philosophy would be right. You would have to do terrible things to stay alive.

Lucy stood over the remains of Akhila, waves of sadness washing over her.

18

It was late afternoon when they reached the distribution warehouse. Lucy put the time at four, maybe five o'clock. The sun was well past its peak for the day, a three-quarter sun, right in between its zenith and the horizon. They were in north Arlington, in an industrial area peppered with large warehouses and small factories looming in the silence. Her internal clock was pushing her to move, move, move.

Things were still in flux; there were still things to do, mitigation efforts to undertake. She could still keep them safe. And there was no question now that Norah was her charge, her ward. At some point, the fluidity would end, things would start to harden. She wanted to have their shit together before the music stopped playing. She did not want to end up without chairs to put their fannies in.

The distribution center sat on an access road that had forked off the main highway. A large sign bearing the name Penumbra Food Group marked the facility's perimeter. In the forefront stood a handful of smaller outbuildings guarding the main facility deeper in the campus. The parking lot was empty, and the grass was on the shaggy side. It was quiet except for the susurration of the grasses in the afternoon breeze. Lucy gestured to her companions; she took a knee behind a low brick wall fronting the property. Eric and Manny slid in behind her.

Even at a fraction of its capacity, the place would be a virtual gold mine. An ordinary grocery store had enough dry and canned goods to support a single individual for years; a distribution warehouse was exponentially larger than even the biggest grocery store. Even better was that this facility was off the beaten path; its existence wouldn't be common knowledge, at least relative to the typical convenience store or supermarket. Even the 'folks who worked here wouldn't have easy access to it; most of the employees would not have lived nearby, and the journey to get here would be fraught with danger. And even if others had already started helping themselves to the warehouse's bounty, there would be enough for scores of looters. The place could keep them fed for a long time.

"What are you doing?" asked Eric.

"It's called reconnaissance," she said. "We don't know if anybody's here, do we?"

She said it condescendingly, intentionally so. She wanted Eric to know that it wasn't his way or the highway. That she knew what she was talking about and that he did not.

She poked her head over the lip of the sign and studied the campus. She scanned the rooftops, the sides of the buildings, the windows, looking for any sign of life. Nothing.

"You got that gun ready?"

Eric nodded. His face was tight with fear. A look with which she'd become intimately familiar. She'd seen it in the face of every new grunt headed out on their first patrol. This was probably a lot different than Eric had imagined during his fantasies of shootouts and street warfare.

Lucy emerged from the cover of the wall and crept toward the first building; Eric and Manny fell in behind her. She paused at the first building, a prefabricated trailer. She jiggled the doorknob. Locked. Probably not much worth scavenging in there anyway.

"Main building," she whispered.

Up ahead was a loading dock. The bay doors, sixteen of them, were all shut. There were no trucks, which struck Lucy as odd. Debris was scattered along the road fronting the dock. Cardboard boxes, twine, dollies. A flutter of discomfort tickled Lucy's stomach; it felt like she was missing something important. The phrase '*it was quiet, TOO quiet*' flashed across her brain like a Times Square marquee.

Her first thought was an imminent ambush. Perhaps her eye had caught movement, hidden, furtive movement, but her brain hadn't had time to process it yet. A group may have already occupied the facility and were readying a counterstrike against three idiots who couldn't see the forest for the trees. What if, in their desperation, they had underestimated what people would do to survive?

She hustled across a strip of asphalt and took cover behind a white pickup truck with a Penumbra Foods logo on the door. Eric and Manny followed suit, apparently picking up on Lucy's sudden anxiety. Manny's face was pale with fear. Eric's eyes were prowling, prowling, prowling.

"Something's not right," she whispered.

"Don't you puss out on me now," Eric snapped. "We need food."

Her gut was screaming. Something was wrong, but she couldn't distill the psychic flora in her gut into useful data. That was the problem with your gut. Sometimes, it sounded an alarm, but it didn't tell you what the alarm was for. And she didn't see any evidence of a hidden threat here. The place looked abandoned, a ghost town. There just didn't appear to be anyone here. No evidence of human activity, something she'd been trained to spot while in the Army. It made finding a place to administer battlefield care easier. She didn't want to give up the warehouse on nothing more than a hunch.

"I'm gonna do a loop of the perimeter," she said. "You keep an eye out. Can you guys whistle loudly?"

Eric nodded.

"You see anything, do a bird call, just two notes, as loudly as you can. Got it?"

Eric nodded again.

She cupped his chin in her hand.

"You listen to me good now," Lucy said.

"What?"

"If there's trouble, I need you to cover me with that gun. Just like you did at the gas station."

"I got you."

"I can take it off your hands."

"I got it," he snapped.

She let out a sigh. It would have to do. For now, at least, they were united in purpose. They needed the same thing. And if there was trouble here, then he could live out his apocalyptic fantasies and save the girl.

"Manny, you good?"

"Yeah. You be careful."

She squeezed his shoulder.

"I'll be fine."

She gave the vicinity a final once-over and then bolted from her hiding spot. It took her less than ten seconds to cover the fifty yards to the building's exterior, but it felt like an hour. Here, she was most exposed, and she waited for the staccato of hidden gunfire to bring her down. But fifty yards became half that and then half again, and then she was there, slamming into the safety of the wall. The desperate sprint had left her sweating and breathing heavily. She waited until her breathing returned to normal before making her next move. She wiped her hands on her shorts.

For a moment, she felt disoriented. It was a Sunday

afternoon and instead of catching up on her sleep or reading a book or harvesting the early spring vegetables on the farm with her brother, she was literally fighting for her life. Lucy Goodwin knew better than most how your life could change forever in an instant, but this was hard to swallow.

She began a loop of the L-shaped building, keeping close to the wall, keeping her eyes peeled. The air was thick with humidity and pressed down on her like a heavy blanket. Blackbirds squawked loudly overhead. A pair of squirrels chased each other in a circle around the parking lot. For Mother Earth's non-human children, it was just another day. No skin off their back. It was kind of funny if you thought about it. For all their advancements, for all their ingenuity, humans, the top of the food chain for tens of thousands of years, had the farthest to fall. They'd painted themselves into this technological corner. Meanwhile, those two squirrels, with brains no bigger than a peanut, would weather the coming storm just fine.

She reached the interior angle of the L and then made her way to its tip, passing an empty loading dock along the way. This struck her as odd; she would have expected to see at least some loading bays serviced by tractor trailers. Perhaps they had just finished a load-out or load-in shortly before the Pulse hit.

As she considered this oddity, this thread hanging loose from the fabric of her current mission, a single gunshot splintered the afternoon silence. It was close, very close, no more than a hundred yards away. She listened for Eric's bird call, but none came. She waited for additional gunfire, but again there was silence. She was on the far side of the building now, out of Eric and Manny's line of sight. Behind her, the coast remained clear.

Her heart was pounding now. She was unarmed and flying blindly. Calling out to Manny or Eric wasn't an option, lest she give away her position. Her only choice was to keep moving to the next corner of the building and hopefully get a look back toward her point of origin. She passed by a window, but it was too dark inside to see anything. At the next corner, she paused again and peered around the side, looking south toward the main entrance. Neither Eric nor Manny were visible. Her worry grew exponentially; she was in terrible danger now, she was certain of it. And if she were in danger, then by extension, so was Norah.

A pair of doors set into a small vestibule lay about ten yards ahead. After another quick check, she bolted for the cover of the vestibule, taking cover against the short wall closest to the door. Again, she checked for possible threats, still seeing none. The setting sun was in her face, but more importantly, it shone inside the warehouse. Out here, she was exposed; she preferred her chances inside, where there would be hiding places and items that could serve as weapons. Hell, even a can of black beans would come in handy.

She carefully pulled the door open, a little bit at a time, revealing a growing sliver of inky darkness. Once again, the reality of a world without electricity slammed home. It was deathly silent. He eyes slowly adjusted to the darkness while the sunshine chewed away the edges of the inky void. Silhouettes of shelving as far as the eye could see floated in the darkness. She took a few steps inside.

The scene brightened in the sun setting behind her, revealing empty shelving.

She stared at them for a moment, unable to process what she was seeing. Row after row of bare shelves.

The warehouse was empty.

Then it hit her.

It was a trap.

Eric had set them up.

19

Lucy froze.

Another gunshot rang out, shattering the cinderblock just above her head. Debris bit at her face like concrete hornets. It galvanized her, sending her scampering inside the building. She moved deeper into the gloom, pausing at the windows. They were too high for her to see through, so she improvised. The shelving was sturdy; she grabbed a post and hoisted herself up onto the second row of shelves, which gave her a decent view across the parking lot, including the spot where she had left Manny and Eric. The shadows seemed longer than they had just a few minutes ago. It felt like the light of the day was dying, a candle flickering out.

Neither man was at the rally point.

But just a few steps to the east, a figure lay prone on the ground. It looked like Manny. His shirt was discolored. A dark puddle had collected underneath him.

Manny was dead.

How could she have been so stupid?

She racked her brain, trying to understand Eric's treachery. Clearly, they had something Eric wanted. Perhaps Angela wanted it too. The trick was figuring out what it was. And then it hit her. It was so brutally obvious, so horrifyingly apparent that it had never occurred to her.

They wanted Norah.

The whole gambit had been to separate Norah from Lucy and Manny. Lucy didn't need to know *why* they wanted Norah; there would be no good answer to that question. The important part was that they now had her.

That was where Eric had gone that morning. To work out the details of his plan.

She hopped down to the ground, now on full alert. Eric was hunting her. She edged her way to the door, taking care with each step. Every inch was fraught with risk. Her head was on a swivel, prepared for any attack. Her soldierly instincts were coming back to life, perhaps a bit more slowly than she might have preferred but returning nevertheless. Hard to believe how rusty those skills became with disuse. She had to put herself back on a wartime footing and stay on it until this crisis ended. Which, she was fully realizing, didn't look to be anytime soon.

Back at the vestibule, she scanned the area again. Eric was nowhere to be found. She scooted across the parking lot and ducked behind an industrial trash container.

From there, she had a clear line of sight toward Manny. Her friend Manny. Now dead. He was lying on his stomach, his arms pinned underneath his body. There appeared to be a small entry wound just above the nape of his neck. He had likely never seen it coming; a brush of cold metal at his skull, and that had been that. Lucy pressed her body against the metal skin of the trash bin. Well, now she knew why Eric hadn't wanted her to have a gun.

That was when she remembered that Eric had not wanted her tagging along on this little mission in the first place. If that were the case, then maybe he had intended her to suffer the same fate as Norah. Which meant that she was lucky to be alive. But she had insisted on coming, and it would have raised suspicion if he had been insistent in his refusal. But why drag them all the way to this God-forsaken corner of town to get rid of Manny?

Deniability.

Out here, Manny's death would be one of countless others, collateral damage of the Pulse. Crimes that had been committed since it happened would likely go unpunished, even when things got back on track. There just wouldn't be enough resources to bring all the guilty to justice.

And to the extent Eric had a master plan, it had not gone off without a hitch. Even highwaymen dealt with hassle. He'd probably wanted to kill them both earlier, but he had bided his time a little too long; the price for his inaction was that she was now onto him.

Whatever had brought them to this point was now irrelevant. She had the pressing matter of staying alive to attend to. She was safe for the moment, but if she left the cover of the Dumpster, she would be badly exposed. If Eric was even a half-decent shot, he could cut her down without too much trouble, and there was no telling where he might be hiding.

"Come out, come out, wherever you are," Eric called out in an exaggerated southern drawl.

His voice was coming from everywhere and nowhere; the acoustical nightmare that was the Dumpster made it difficult to get a bead on his location.

"You got two choices," he said. "You can die here or give yourself up."

His voice boomed in the afternoon stillness, flushing a small flock of blackbirds from a nearby oak tree. The susurration of their wings flapping deadened the echo of his voice.

She remained dead silent.

What she would not have given for a gun right then. She swore to herself that if she survived this little predicament, she would never again be unarmed. She had liked not having to carry a gun; it was one of the great things about America. That's what people didn't understand. There was a weight to carrying a gun, and it ate at you. Because a gun served one purpose and one purpose only. To terminate life. And before the Pulse, the odds you would ever have needed one were statistically zero. In other countries, corrupt countries where no one could count on the police or the military to protect them, that's where you needed guns.

No more.

For now, those days were over.

But first, Norah.

She had to find Norah.

Leaving her with Angela had been a terrible decision; if Lucy were lucky, it was not yet one that had cost the girl her life. Lucy had made the mistake of believing her interests were aligned with those of Eric and Angela simply because they were staying under the same roof, albeit temporarily. But Eric had been a step ahead of her; the failure to recognize that burned hot inside her. But she had been given a second chance. She could correct her mistake if she played her cards correctly. There would be risk. Everything going forward would be fraught with risk.

Step one was getting back to the house.

She needed to follow Eric back; the only way to do that was to convince him she'd escaped and then trail him back to the house once he'd given up. It would be excruciating work. Tailing someone was extraordinarily difficult. And Eric had a good set of instincts on him, she had to admit.

She broke from the cover of the Dumpster, making a beeline back toward the building, staying in shadow where she could. Her lithe frame ensured her footfalls were virtually silent; it was a habit she'd picked up in the hospital, moving quickly but quietly so as not to bother resting patients. She made it safely to the east side of the building, drawing no additional fire. Back inside, she wound her way deeper into the building, looking for the roof access.

She hugged the inside perimeter of the darkened warehouse, moving slowly but efficiently, brushing her hands along the walls as she had inside Tim's high school. That seemed like a lifetime ago. She hoped that Tim was making do; she wondered how long their food supply would last. Once that ran out, there would be very little to keep the kids anchored to the place.

She came to a doorway. She pushed gently on the metal handle, unlatching it. Then she pushed it open slowly, just enough to squeeze through the gap. The door closed quietly, leaving her alone in a pitch-black stairwell. An exploring foot found the first step, and she slowly made her way up. Sweat lacquered her back, gluing her shirt to her skin. At the landing, she paused and took a breath before finishing the climb up the next flight. She pushed open the door at the top of the stairwell, revealing the rooftop beyond. A warm but refreshing breeze blew across her, cooling her skin. She blocked the door with a cinderblock at her foot.

The rooftop was bigger than she'd expected, covering the area of several football fields. There were a number of roof accesses, at least six by her count. She made her way to the edge as the afternoon made its turn toward evening. She wouldn't have much time to locate Eric before it got too dark. A gentle breeze was blowing, carrying with it the acrid scent of smoke. The day was clear; she could see a couple of miles in any direction. Interstate 66 shimmered in the late afternoon sunset, the sea of abandoned steel reflecting the bright sunshine.

On her first scan of the complex, Eric was nowhere to be seen. At least six buildings dotted the campus, more than she initially had thought. There were more alleys and blind corners than she could count. In her head, she broke up the campus into six grids, studying each one carefully before moving to the next one. For the first three, not a flicker of movement. But on the fourth, a flicker. At first, she thought it was just haze shimmering from the blacktop. But it was Eric edging his way down an alley, his gun up like he was in an episode of *Miami Vice*.

He made his way up and down each alley, cursing more loudly with each step. When his search ended fruitlessly, he stood in the midway, a hand on his hip. He seemed to be considering his next move. Then he raised his gun up in the air and squeezed off three quick shots, screaming an angry, guttural bellow as he did.

BANG! BANG! BANG!

That's right, you miserable asshole. You'll never find me.

She wondered if he would search each building one by one, if he would attempt to be thorough. As he should. Part of her wanted him to just so she could shove him over the edge, watch his arms and legs windmill as he plummeted to a date with the asphalt below. But she needed him alive. She needed him alive and back at the house; if he went missing, that might put Norah in even more danger.

His shoulders sagged, perhaps indicating he was giving up his search for Lucy. She watched him move south toward the complex's main entrance. She waited until he reached the access road, where he turned east, back the way they had come. Once she had a bead on his heading, she left her perch at the roof and quickly made her way back down the stairs. Taking care to close the doors quietly, she moved quickly down the midway, turning east.

She wanted to kill Eric, but she could not yet. It'd been a long time since she'd killed anyone. A month before her last tour in Iraq ended. She had been on perimeter duty that afternoon. It had been a quiet shift. Shortly before dinner, her partner spotted a local approaching from the west. Immediately, they both knew he was trouble. He had olive skin, and his head was heavy with black, curly hair. She didn't recognize him, which was the first warning sign. Her platoon interacted with many of the locals, who gave them intelligence about the terror cells in the area and brought them pastries and other sweets from time to time.

She immediately raised her M4 rifle into a firing position and ordered the man to turn around and go back home. She'd already mentally marked the redline that he could not cross; it was a rusted coal oil drum. But she knew that he was not going to stop. He didn't even look at them.

She sighted the target and squeezed off a quick burst. Her aim was pure and the fusillade blew apart the man's head. He was holding a deadman switch, and when he let go, his vest exploded. It was a total fluke. A rock kicked up by the blast wave caught her partner in the throat and ruptured his carotid artery. He bled to death before they could get the first medic to him.

Like she had that day, she had revenge on her mind.

It didn't take long to pick up Eric's trail. He fired off a fourth shot from his weapon; the report of the shot matched the three he had let loose back at the warehouse. He was loud and angry, cursing, kicking over trash cans, shattering windshields of abandoned cars.

She finally spotted him at an intersection about a hundred yards ahead. She was at a good distance here, close enough to keep tabs on him but not too close that he would notice her.

She followed.

20

Eric moved at a glacial pace, taking shortcuts and ducking into various storefronts to scavenge. As she trailed the man, she thought about her dream from the night before. It had been about Emma. As usual. Emma. Emma. Her whole life. It wasn't fair. She should be here, and it wasn't fair that she wasn't. She could have taken care of Emma in a situation like this. It wouldn't have been like cancer, when she'd had no control over anything.

Lucy been at the beach in the dream, no idea which beach or how she'd gotten there, as was the case with dreams. She heard Emma calling for her.

Mommy.

Whozat.

Mommy.

Nope.

It wasn't her.

Her head hurt.

She blinked.

It was very bright. The light was too bright. How did people walk around with their eyes open all the time? Even with her eyes closed, the sun's rays blasted her pupils with harsh, hot, angry light. Even with her eyes closed, the light made her head hurt.

Mommy!

Emma.

Emma!

She sat up, but she couldn't see anything but white, a blinding white light as far as the eye could see. Like sitting in traffic facing the setting sun when you couldn't get the visor just right, and you couldn't see past the hood of your car.

Mommy.

Kids, man, kids. They called on you relentlessly, demanding every last second you had in service of them. But that was wrong, it was all wrong because Emma was gone and was not there to make demands on her time. She hated having free time to herself, and she hated it when other mothers complained about having no time to themselves because of their kids even if they were joking.

Because there was no one to make demands on her time.

So why was someone calling her *Mommy*?

Not anymore.

Mommy.

It was someone else's kid here on this beach with its

white sand and white hot light. Even the water was white like molten lead, reflecting back the light of that white hot sun.

She looked around for the child and her incessant call for her Mommy.

Dammit, woman, look up from your phone and listen to your damn kid. Don't be looking at your damn phone while she drowns.

Mommy.

She even sounded like Emma.

That was cruel, coming to the beach to get some peace and quiet and to hear a sweet, little voice that sounded like Emma's. It wasn't anyone's fault that she sounded like Emma. But it still hurt.

Mommy, wake up.

Lucy froze. That didn't sound *like* Emma's voice.

That *was* Emma's voice.

Mommy, wake up.

There was a figure standing before her, silhouetted in the light, a negative, an un-person, blackness carved from the light. An Emma-shaped void. She shook her head, trying to clear the cobwebs, but that triggered another wave of pain shimmering through her. She felt nauseated.

It couldn't be Emma.

Emma was gone.

The odds had been in their favor until they weren't. The treatment was working until it wasn't. She was progressing nicely until she wasn't. Emma had died of a disease that she'd had a seventy percent chance of surviving.

The chemo had been terrible, wrecking Emma's tiny frame as the chemicals had done their work, microscopic assassins hunting and destroying the rogue cells that were trying to kill Emma. Nausea, hair loss, the whole nine yards. Emma slept eighteen, twenty hours a day; Lucy sat next to her in bed, watching her sleep or scouring the internet for the latest treatment options for childhood leukemia. She read the same websites over and over; she didn't even know why she did it. She was going to follow the doctors' advice.

Then the first ten days of chemo were over. Slowly, life returned to normal. Her hair started to grow back, her energy returned slowly, and hints of the old Emma began to resurface. Her appetite returned, and Lucy made her favorite foods. Quesadillas and chicken tenders and peanut butter and honey sandwiches. Chocolate milk and fruit punch. Caesar salads literally drowning in dressing. They tried not to think about the next block; they just focused on the now, that she had done it, that she had fought this terrible battle and won it.

But before they knew it, the second round of chemo was upon them, the thirty days in between sessions blowing by in the blink of an eye. The second round was even worse than the first. Emma hadn't completely recovered from the first bout of chemo, and there were days that Lucy wasn't sure Emma's body would hold out.

But held out she had, and she was done.

The night before the results came back, neither of
them could sleep. Emma was still too young to understand life and death, but she knew that something had to
be terribly wrong if the medicine that was supposed to fix
her made her sicker than she'd ever felt in her life. They
sat up playing board games and watching movies.

Then before they knew it, they were sitting in the
doctor's office. Doctors' private offices were strange to
Lucy; each one was designed to the physician's personal
tastes, very different from the antiseptic sameness of
examination rooms and surgical wards. Weird that she
would receive the most critical news of her life in this
room with the baseball theme, decked out with Washington Nationals memorabilia, framed sports pages,
commemorative baseballs.

The doctor reviewed the chart one last time, which
bothered Lucy; it was like he was squeezing in a little last-
minute cramming before a big test. This was her daughter's goddamn life on the line. He should have her results
committed to memory (even though as a nurse she knew
that to be unrealistic). But she wasn't here as a nurse; she
was here as a mom.

He looked up and removed his reading glasses.

"It's good news," he said, a broad smile spreading
across his face.

They went out for pizza, and Lucy took Emma to her
favorite little bookstore in town, which she'd left with an
armful of new books to read while she recovered. The
next day, they took the train (the train, the train, why was

she thinking about trains? It was like seeing someone you thought you knew just out of the corner of your eye, but then you look again, and they're gone) to Washington, D.C., and saw the sights. It was late March, and the cherry blossoms had been in bloom; the entire city popped with color like it was giving off its own light. Emma had liked the Spy Museum the best. They stayed at the Waldorf on 16th Street, which cost Lucy a fortune, but she didn't care. They were the best two days of her life.

It was going to be okay.

Which was why it had hurt so badly when the cancer came back.

mommy wake up mommy wake up mommy wake up mommy wake up

LUCY SNAPPED BACK TO REALITY.

They were back at the shopping strip, back at Manny's post-hangover pizza joint. It was full dark now and had been for some time, which had made it easier to follow him under the soft, shimmery light of a gibbous moon. Plus, he covered his tracks with all the stealth of a car bomb. She lingered behind a bush as he disappeared behind the shopping center.

There was comfort here after the haunted funhouse of the world beyond. It felt good to be thinking more than one step ahead for the first time since this disaster had happened. Just to get back to the house and find out what had happened to Norah.

She hoped the kid was still alive.

Please let her be alive.

Please let it not be too late.

Because if she were dead, it would have been Lucy's fault. Her failure to read the situation. If she could just get to Norah, get her out of this mess, she wouldn't make this mistake again.

No sir.

Not again.

She crossed the street and hid behind a corner of the strip mall. Eric's silhouetted figure continued ambling toward the house; she crept down the street toward the trees flanking the side street feeding the neighborhood. The cul-de-sac was mostly silent but for the soft murmur of conversation. Some people would have their windows open for the breeze. Not everyone though. In the windows of the houses, candles and lanterns burned, their flickering coronas throwing spooky shadows against the curtains drawn tight against the outside. The carnival atmosphere from the first night was a distant memory. It was becoming real for them. Maybe not as real as it had already become for her, but real enough.

Eric had made it to the house.

"Angela!" he called out, his voice bellowing across the neighborhood.

Lucy scampered behind a minivan parked in the circle three doors away from Angela's, kneeling at the right rear bumper. The clatter of Angela unlatching the chain filled the air; the door swung open, creaking loudly on its hinges, and Eric slipped inside. There had been no sign of Norah.

Lucy was alone on the street. No one was outside. A moment later, she heard Eric's voice again, slipping through the open windows. He was angry and loud. She zipped from the cover of the minivan and across the yard. There was a row of thick boxwoods fronting the house; she wedged herself in between the bushes and the house's exterior walls. The thick branches scratched and tore at her skin, but she was well concealed. It would be virtually impossible for anyone to spot her.

"What happened?" Angela was asking, her voice desperate. "Where's everyone else?"

"Doesn't matter," he said. "Did Simon come?"

"Yeah," Angela said.

"When?"

"A while ago. It was still light out."

"Did he ask about her?"

"I told him what you told me to say."

"Good," Eric said. "Good."

"Please tell me what happened."

"We got jumped. Your friend Manny got shot."

"Oh my God. They're dead?"

"Sorry, babe. I know you were friends."

"What about Lucy?"

"We got separated. I don't know."

She sobbed.

"Look at it this way, babe," he said. "He can't cause any more trouble for us when things go back to normal."

Lucy went red with rage. This man was a monster, and Angela wasn't much better. A cost-benefit analysis of Manny's death. But Norah. Where was Norah? What had this psychopath done with her? Eric's plan was coming into focus. Eric was using them as currency. He understood the increasingly dire situation and he was acting on that understanding. Simon, whoever he was, would trade supplies for her and Norah. That had been the plan all along until she had forced her way into the supply run with Manny. He'd had to let her join them; if he'd pushed back, she would have grown suspicious.

"Did you get any food?"

"Dammit, Ang, does it look I got any food?"

This silenced the nurse.

"Now what?"

"Tomorrow, we're gonna go collect."

21

The house grew quieter over the next hour. The candles in the house darkened one by one as Eric and Angela retired for the night. A burst of an argument between the couple broke the silence, as did the quick bout of loud sex that followed, making for an extremely uncomfortable five minutes. Then things were calm once more. Eventually, the sound of snoring echoed through the house. Whoever it was had a severe case of sleep apnea. Maybe it was Eric; with any luck, it would soon kill him.

Lucy crept around the side of the house, taking care with each step, and into the backyard through the side gate. The yard was small, maybe a few hundred square feet. As far as northern Virginia yards went, it was virtually an estate. The remains of what had once been a garden, now overrun with weeds, occupied the northwest corner. A wooden bench sat under the yard's lone tree in the middle of the yard. Neither was a particularly good place to camp out for the night. She edged the length of the yard, staying close to the house as she did so.

The deeper incursion yielded results. There was a prefabricated shed in the corner opposite the garden. Lucy carefully drew open the door; a breath of humid, musty air greeted her. She positioned the doors to keep herself concealed while still giving her a view of the house. She took a deep breath and exhaled slowly. Her body was caked with a thin film of sweat and grime. She would have given her left hand for a shower. But that would have to wait; she had work to do.

The night stretched interminably. She dozed. She dreamed about Emma and then she was awake and it was still dark. Overhead, clouds streamed underneath a moonless night like ships on an ocean of stars.

She thought about Simon.

Simon, Simon, Simon.

She needed to figure out who he was and where he was. Someone above Eric's paygrade in whatever criminal enterprise he was involved in. A man who trafficked in human beings. It didn't take a genius to figure out what Norah would be used for. Lucy could not let that happen. She would not let that happen.

Sleep overtook her once more, and she dozed until the first hint of dawn, the blackness of the night softening into purple. She crept across the yard while she still had the cover of darkness, discovering a hidden set of stairs descending to a basement. It could be a good place to hide and gather intel. After ensuring the coast around her was clear, she descended the steps quickly. The basement door was unlocked; the knob squealed as she turned it, freezing her in place. But the house remained quiet.

The basement was dim and musty and, like the rest of the house, stank of cigarette smoke and booze. There was a workbench crowded with various household supplies on the far wall. Bleach, laundry detergent, bottles of spray cleaner. To her right stood a small washer and dryer and a basket of dirty clothes. A pegboard hanging on the wall to her left was home to an array of tools. Using the dim but increasing light through the window, Lucy studied the selections, settling on a hand trowel. She carefully removed it from the anchor, comforted by the weight of the small weapon. In the absence of her own gun, that and the knife would make for a fearsome combination.

As the day brightened, Angela and Eric began to stir. His heavy footsteps echoed loudly in the basement. There was just nothing subtle about him. Angela's footsteps were much daintier and more frequent. He barked at her constantly, treating her like a slave. She took a post at the foot of the stairs, playing the odds that without electricity, there would be no reason for either of them to venture down this way.

The acoustics of the basement were terrible, and as such, their conversations were muffled, making it difficult to eavesdrop. Occasionally, however, his voice cut through the static like a supernova.

"Angie, get me a beer!"

The crack and hiss of a beer can. Eric and Angela didn't talk much, just some brief chit-chat here and there. She couldn't hear them all that well, and she didn't care to. She had all the information she needed for the time being. Now, she could focus on gleaning the next bit of intelligence: Norah's whereabouts.

Which wasn't to say that it would be easy.

The day drew out like taffy. It was warm in the basement but not terribly so; still, Lucy felt disgusting, her body spackled with the grime of two days of utter chaos. Around midday, one of them lit a joint, filling the air with the pungent tang of weed. This was to Lucy's advantage. The harder they partied, the less attention they would pay to their surroundings. By the time the sun had pushed over the top of the house, leaving the backyard in shadow, Eric had probably plowed through a dozen beers.

Lucy's stomach growled loudly. She had not eaten or drank anything in twenty-four hours. She licked the inside of her wrist, the salty tang of her sweat not unpleasant and somewhat energizing. It wasn't a long-term solution to her hydration concerns, but it would do for now.

The house had fallen quiet once more. Apparently, even Eric's liver, robust as it was, had its limits. It was probably late afternoon; the heat of the day was subsiding, and it had grown noticeably cooler in the basement. There was still usable light left in the sky, maybe two hours' worth. Lucy thought about Norah, about how scared the girl must have been, how betrayed she must have felt. Lucy could not let her down, could not abandon her to these monsters. But she was no closer to learning anything new. Norah's whereabouts remained a mystery.

As she considered her next move, she heard a new sound echoing through the house. The metronomic thumping continued for a few seconds and then stopped. Then it resumed, a bit more frantically. Someone was knocking on the door.

"Who is it?" barked Eric.

Panic rippled from Lucy's stomach to her throat. She was running out of time. It was would've been hard enough to take on Eric and Angela alone; she would have no chance if they had allies joining them this evening. She edged her way up the staircase, two steps from the zenith; the doorknob was just barely within her reach.

The reply from the other side of the door was inaudible.

She had to make her move now. As best as she could recall, the basement door opened up on the back hallway near the kitchen. With Angela and Eric distracted by their visitor, now would be her chance. She slowly turned the knob and opened the door an inch at a time; the kitchen was dark and empty. She stepped into the kitchen, carefully closing the door behind her. She held the trowel tightly in her right hand. She would attack Eric first, disable him with the knife, get the gun away from him.

She eased her way down the corridor, one step at a time, sliding her feet together and then spreading them apart. Her back was pressed against the wall, out of the main line of sight of the living room.

Whispers from the living room. She could not make out the words.

She edged closer to the end of the hallway, as far as she could go without giving away her position. She could see half of the living room, the back half; the other half, including the entrance foyer, remained out of her line of sight.

The door opened.

"What do you want?" barked Eric.

The voice was still muffled, but she could hear it a bit more clearly. The voice was familiar to her, but she could not quite place it. Her brain cycled through voiceprints stored on its hard drive, looking, looking, looking.

"Just wanted to check on Ang."

Click.

Oh shit.

It was Tim Whitaker, their port in a storm at the high school. She wanted to scream out, to warn him. His life was in immediate danger and he had no idea.

"We're fine," Eric snapped.

Just leave, she pleaded silently.

She did not want Eric to know that Tim had crossed paths with her and Norah. Nothing good would come from that.

"Okay," Tim replied.

There was an awkward silence. She pictured him turning back down the walkway, away from this nightmare. He didn't deserve to walk into this hornet's nest.

No such luck.

"Well, I came all this way, and it was a hell of a trip," he said. "Mind if I say hey to Angela before I head back?"

"Yeah, I guess so," Eric said.

Angela stepped from the shadows of the family room, just off Eric's left hip.

"Hey, Tim," she said.

"Hey, yourself."

Lucy's heart was breaking. The girl was bad news, and Tim very likely knew it at a rational level, but he couldn't help himself. He had walked miles through a broken world that was coming apart at the seams just to check on her. He still loved her. The heart wanted what it wanted. Love. Stupid, pointless, heartbreaking love. Stupid, possibly fatal love.

Okay, Timmy, you had your awkward hello, now turn around and mosey on back to the high school.

"Hey, one other thing before I go..."

No, no, no, no.

"What?"

Eric again.

"I met a friend of yours a few days ago," he said. "Manny? There was a woman with him. They make it here?"

"No," Eric said.

"Huh," he said. "Hope they're okay."

"He and Lucy never made it here."

Lucy's heart was pounding.

Tim made a clicking noise with his tongue.

"Okay then."

The door began to close.

"Hey," Tim said. The door's flight was interrupted by his hand.

"What?"

"How'd you know her name was Lucy?"

"What?"

"I never said her name."

Oh shit.

"What?" Eric said a second time.

"Angela, what's going on?" Tim said.

Angela remained silent.

"They were here, weren't they?" Tim said, a hint of fear spicing his voice. He had no idea what was going on, but it was obvious he knew something was terribly wrong. "Where are they?"

"Look man, I don't know what you're talking about," Eric said, anger edging into his voice. "Get out of here before you piss me off."

Lucy could wait no longer.

She burst from the shadows, her trowel at the ready. Eric's hands had dropped to the small of his back; he was going for a weapon. Tim was in mortal danger now.

"Lucy?" he called out. "Manny?"

Eric grabbed Tim by the collar and yanked him inside. Eric was much bigger than the bookish teacher and held the advantage in strength and the element of surprise. He delivered a right cross to Tim's jaw and then threw him to the ground like a child's toy. The commotion covered Lucy's approach. She reared back and stepped into a mighty swing of the trowel, aiming it directly at Eric's head. She missed his skull, but the tool's three prongs buried themselves deep in his upper back. He howled in agony as three roses of blood blossomed on his damp T-shirt. Although her strike had not dropped him to the ground, the impact had shaken his gun loose and sent it clattering to the ground. He swung his arms wildly, knocking her knife to the ground.

Twilight was setting in now, dropping its curtain on the world, and the house was dark but for the flicker of the candle. Eric remained stunned from the blow, but he would recover quickly. Angela was screaming and crying unintelligibly. Lucy wondered if they would draw the attention of the neighbors or whether they had already reached the *every man for himself* portion of the festivities.

The gun. She had to find the gun.

Already Eric was scanning for it. Lucy dove to the ground, pawing at the carpet like a blind woman. Eric, having sniffed out her gambit, kicked her in the side. Fortunately, it was a glancing blow; if he'd connected head on, he likely would have splintered her rib cage. She might not get as lucky the next time. Tim was on his feet now, desperately swinging at Eric and drawing his fire away from Lucy.

The quartet was careening through the living room

now, crashing into end tables and banging against chairs and sofas. It reminded Lucy of close-quarters battle like she had seen in Iraq. She stayed focused on her objective. The gun was the only thing that mattered. Everything hinged on her finding the gun first.

As the brawl unfolded above her, beneath her, around her, each second was an eternity in itself. A scream of pain, maybe Tim, she didn't know. Angela's incessant screaming, Eric bellowing with rage. Her hands desperately clawed for the gun, fingertips scraping at the threadbare carpet. Another kick to her rib cage, this one a bit squarer than the first.

Then.

A breakthrough. Her fingertips brushed across the cold steel of the barrel. She pushed it ahead of her, under the table for a bit of cover. She rolled over and took aim with the gun, but all she could see was the faint outline of legs lurching to and fro. She crawled in between the table and the couch, aimed toward the ceiling, and pulled the trigger.

The gun roared.

Bits of debris rained down from the ceiling. Tim, Angela, and Eric dove for the ground for cover. Lucy scrambled to her feet, on the high ground now.

"Tim, get up," she said.

Tim complied.

A candle on the table continued flickering, throwing shadows against the wall. It had somehow avoided overturning during the melee. Angela cowered on the ground, her hands over her head. She was whimpering. Eric sat crisscrossed with his hands in his lap. The look on his face was pure murder. But he was apparently wise enough not to mess with an enraged ex-soldier pointing a gun at his face.

"Listen to me very carefully," Lucy said. "I'm going to ask one time and one time only. Where is Norah?"

"She's gone."

"Wrong answer."

She kicked Eric in the face, knocking him flat on his back. Blood poured from his nose. She was not taking any shit from this man. Not for a minute, not for a single goddamned second.

"Angela?" she said. "Do you know where she is?"

Angela shook her head. Lucy wasn't sure whether to believe her, but she would deal with Angela later. She might not know the whole story, but she knew something. The key for now was getting Eric to break. If she could break him, then Angela would quickly follow.

"Tim, get me a chair from the kitchen."

She kept the gun trained on Eric while they waited for Tim to return with the chair. She couldn't believe how badly she wanted to shoot this man. There was no second-guessing herself. She had to stop herself from pulling the trigger. He was human garbage. People like Eric curdled the pot of civilization. The only thing stopping her was that he held information on Norah's whereabouts. And as God was her witness, if he wasn't forthcoming with said information, she would happily put a bullet in his brain. Justice for Manny. The only justice Manny would likely ever get.

"Get in the chair," she ordered Eric.

"Fuck you."

She held the gun against his foot and pulled the trigger. The bullet shattered the metatarsals in his foot, shredding muscle and tissue.

Eric screamed in agony.

"You bitch, you fucking shot me," he howled.

"Get in the goddamned chair," she said. "I'm not asking again."

She pressed the gun, still warm from its discharge, to his forehead.

"Now."

"Eric, just listen to her!" Angela shrieked.

He complied silently, climbing into his chair while favoring his injured foot. Shooting him had not bothered her at all. Some people you didn't negotiate with. Some people were malignancies, hell-bent on infecting the world around them. Norah's life was in danger, and she did not have time to play nicely. If there was a reckoning to be had, then she would face it.

"Angela, do you have duct tape?"

She nodded.

"Get it for me. Now."

She left the room, leaving Lucy with the gun trained on Eric. It took every last bit of willpower not to shoot him in the face.

"Tape him to the chair," she said to Tim when Angela

returned with the tape. "Use it all. Arms behind him. Over his thighs and under the chair."

As Tim turned for the tape, Eric leapt out of his chair; Lucy fired the gun but missed badly. She sidestepped Eric, whose significant injuries had weakened him badly as he charged at her, and fired again. This one struck him in the abdomen; he staggered to his left and crashed into the cushions of the loveseat. He rolled off the edge of the chair and crashed onto the ground, face up. He did not move. At such close range, the gunshot had been devastating; blood rapidly pooled underneath him.

The room fell silent, the report of the gunshot still echoing in her ears. Despair flooded through her. Eric had been her sole link to Norah; now he was dead. Angela fell to Eric's side, wailing with grief. Despite everything, despite all this man had shown her to be, she mourned the loss of her partner. Lucy hated her for it.

"You didn't have to shoot him!" she howled, her voice choked with tears.

Lucy ignored her.

"Angela, do you know where Norah is?"

"Get out! Get out of my house!"

"Do you know where Norah is?"

"No!" she screeched, her arms wrapped daintily around Eric's lifeless head.

"Who's Simon?"

"Get out!"

Lucy had had just about enough of Angela's shit. She yanked the woman to her feet by her collar and virtually threw her into the chair Eric had just vacated. Lucy's sudden display of force had silenced the woman.

"Angela, where is Norah?"

She shook her head.

"Are you telling me the truth?"

She nodded unconvincingly.

The woman was lying.

She picked the candle up off the table.

"Tim, hold her arms behind her back."

In the dim orange glow of the tiny corona of flame, Angela's face fell.

Tim looked up at Lucy with surprise. She could see it in the man's face; he didn't have it in him to do what needed to be done. Not yet anyway. But she did.

"Don't worry," she said, acknowledging his hesitation. "Angela won't let it get that far."

She turned her attention back to Angela.

"Right? You're not going to hold back information, are you?"

"He'll kill me."

"Who will? Simon?"

She nodded vigorously.

"*I'll* kill you if you hold anything back."

Lucy's warning froze her.

"Nothing, and I mean nothing, matters more than finding that little girl," Lucy said. "Do you understand me?"

A subtle nod from Angela.

"Now, tell me about Simon."

"He's bad news."

"That's really not very helpful, Angela."

"He's a bad dude," she said. "Big dealer."

"Drugs?"

"Guns, too."

"Keep going," she said. "I want to know everything you know."

"He and Eric met in jail," she said. "Couple years ago. Eric started doing collections for him."

"So Eric worked for him?"

"Kind of."

"Does he live nearby?"

"I don't know."

Lucy drew the candle close to Angela's face.

"I swear I don't know," she said again, her eyes wide and wet with tears.

"Where does he hang out?"

Her eyes cut toward Eric's body as though he could still hurt her.

"There's a bar he owns," she said. "At the Ballston Mall."

"How far is that?"

"Three, four miles," Tim interjected.

"You know the place she's talking about?"

"Which bar?" Tim asked. "Snyder's?"

Angela nodded.

Tim whistled softly.

"Yeah, I know it," he said, shaking his head in apparent disbelief. "Pretty upscale place."

"And what are they gonna do with her?" Lucy said to Angela. "With Norah?"

Angela shook her head.

"You traded her, right? For supplies?"

Angela burst into tears.

"Eric said we had no choice. We're out of food, and the stores are all empty."

An overwhelming urge to strangle Angela right there in her living room gripped Lucy hard. She closed her eyes and waited for the rage to pass. She needed to save it for the ones who truly deserved her ire. The ones who now held Norah.

"She's a child!" Lucy screamed in Angela's face.

Angela cried harder.

"I know," she said over and over. Each refrain arrived in between heavy sobs bursting from her like exploding land mines.

"Did Eric have any other guns in the house?"

She nodded.

"In the bedroom," she said, nodding toward the corridor. "On the shelf in the closet."

She nodded toward Tim, who disappeared down the hallway. She heard him rummaging quickly through the closet. He returned bearing a nine-millimeter handgun and a box of ammunition.

Before leaving, they ate. She had a can of spaghetti while Tim ate a tuna sandwich. She wasn't particularly hungry anymore, but she needed the fuel. At this rate, there was no telling when they might eat again.

Angela watched them disinterestedly, putting up no objection. Lucy offered her a plate of food, but she refused. She seemed to be in shock. Lucy did not know what would become of the woman, but that was not her concern right now. She had made her bed, and now she would have to lie in it. It was a harsh observation, but their reality had become harsh overnight.

When they were done, they gathered a handful of supplies and loaded them into a pair of backpacks. As they made their way toward the door, Angela blocked their path.

"What am I supposed to do now?"

Lucy looked at her with contempt.

"I don't know."

"I'm really sorry," Angela said.

"Too late for that now."

She and Tim stepped around the woman and out into the falling darkness.

22

E verything fell away.

Everything but Norah.

Lucy was unconcerned with the dissolution of the world she had known, focused instead singularly on her ward. Norah was her responsibility now. In less than a week, the Pulse had set the world back decades, if not centuries. There would be no one in authority that could help Norah better than she could. The powers-that-be would be focused on the big problems at a macro level. The Norahs of the world would simply become statistics. There was too much to fix, too much to do just to get the nation back on track, working blindly without power while trying to get it back on.

A steady rain was falling as they trekked southwest toward the Ballston Mall. The precipitation was welcome, as it kept the number of looters and other ruffians to a minimum. A strange quiet had settled over the region. It was like a thick blanket. The sounds of nature were there, the cicadas and June bugs that raised Cain every spring.

The Ballston Quarter, or the Ballston Mall, as it was more commonly known before its recent name change, sat in the heart of Arlington, close to the Ballston/Marymount University Metro stop. It was a popular shopping and dining destination, sporting an eclectic mixture of retail and restaurant locations.

As they drew within sight of the mall, the rain lightened to a drizzle before tapering off completely, leaving behind a clear, moonless night. In the absence of artificial light, the sky glowed with starlight. With so many visible in the immense void of night, Lucy understood why their ancestors had named the constellations the way they had. There was so much more to see than they had ever known. Orion's Belt. Taurus. You could see the bull, you could really see it in the darkness.

She and Tim took refuge in a bus stop vestibule near the mall's main entrance. There were more people out here, younger folks mostly. Across the way was an outdoor seating area for an Italian restaurant.

"Where's Snyder's?" she asked Tim.

"Upper level," he replied.

"What's the layout?"

"Nothing special," he said. "Pretty big. Good-sized bar in the middle splits it in two. Lots of televisions."

"Let's do a loop of the mall," she said.

They followed a sidewalk ringing the perimeter of the shopping center. The mall's exterior looked positively medieval. Tiki torches had been placed every twenty yards or so. Armed guards stood at various entry points to the mall. Simon had taken control of the entire facility. It made sense. The mall held a trove of resources, and Simon would want it all. The people who relied on him for work would have come here after the blackout. He likely had reserves of cash, which would be valuable in the absence of electronic payments. If the blackout endured much longer, cash would lose its value as well, as people would revert to a barter-based economy. But for now, cash still had value.

It took an hour to make a complete circuit of the mall's perimeter They passed a sporting goods store, a department store, a new hotel, and a high-end steakhouse before returning to their point of origin at the café's outdoor seating area. There was no telling where Norah might be.

An idea bloomed in Lucy's brain like activated yeast. She did not like the idea, not one bit, but it was probably their best chance to find the girl.

She told Tim.

"You're insane," he said after she'd finished outlining her plan.

"Can you think of a better idea?"

He rubbed his temples with the tips of his fingers.

"No," he said. "You're right. We don't have much time."

She handed him the gun.

"You know how to use this?"

"Not really," he said, wrapping his fingers around the grip.

"I wouldn't worry about it," she said. "It's more of a prop than anything. If this plan works, we won't even need to use it."

He nodded as he stared at the weapon.

"Ready?" she asked.

"I guess so."

Fear buzzed through her. Fear that she would fail. Fear that she would lose Norah like she had lost Emma.

SIX WEEKS after her second round of chemotherapy, Emma moved onto the second phase of her treatment. This involved three more blocks of chemotherapy, designed to deepen the remission and wipe out any cancer cells lingering in her blood. More nausea, more suffering, more misery. As Emma heaved into the small wastebasket, Lucy closed her eyes and told herself it was in service of a greater cause. That soon they would be through this, and they would prevail. It was what kept Lucy tethered to sanity.

It didn't work.

They sat with the doctor, who explained that the cancer had returned, that for all their efforts, the leukemia continued to hold the upper hand. Lucy was close to madness.

That set Emma through a nightmarish two-year

journey of increasingly desperate treatments including radiation therapy, immunological therapy, and finally, the Hail Mary, a stem cell transplant that took place on Emma's tenth birthday. They did a donor drive for a bone marrow match; hundreds of people volunteered, and amazingly, they found a match in a young woman who had just graduated from VCU's nursing school. Lucy thought it was fate that Emma's life might be saved by another nurse.

Spirits were high.

They had cornered the leukemia, pinned it down, and now it was time to obliterate once and for all this terrible invader of Emma's little body. No guarantees, but the doctors were optimistic. She was a strong little girl. Her body just needed an assist.

The surgery had taken six hours. Lucy pictured the healthy stem cells racing to Emma's bone marrow, where they would start producing healthy platelets and red and white blood cells. Taking charge, getting shit done at a microscopic level. It meant wiping out Emma's own immune system, but again, it was a price to pay in furtherance of a greater cause.

She stayed in the hospital for a month, isolated in a clean room. Lucy visited her wearing specially treated masks and gowns. And they waited. They waited alone, she and Emma, watching movies and reading books and doing puzzles, only leaving the clean environment of Lucy's home to visit the doctor. They went stir crazy;

again, it was a sacrifice at the altar of total victory over the leukemia.

Follow-up visit after follow-up visit, six months' worth, before the doctors would be ready to declare her back in remission. They were cautiously optimistic after the first few visits.

They made it four months.

The cancer returned.

Who knew why these things happened? said the doctors. Some illnesses and some patients were just beyond the reach of modern medicine. No, there was nothing else to try. They would try to get her into some experimental treatment protocols, but there was no guarantee they would work *(that she might not even live long enough to try them was the horrible unsaid thing that remained unsaid).*

She could not help Emma no matter how badly she wanted to. She would have lain down her life for Emma, but that and six dollars wouldn't have gotten her anything but a fancy coffee.

But she could do something to help Norah. She could give everything for Norah.

She could die for Norah.

She *would* die for Norah.

TIM ESCORTED her to the main entrance, his hand at her elbow, the gun pressed into her ribcage. A tall, skinny man guarding the door, standing in the glow of the tiki torch, held up his hand.

"Who the hell are you?" he asked, raising his weapon. It looked like an AR-15.

Tim took a deep breath and let it out slowly.

"Eric sent me," he said, tipping his head toward Lucy. "Told me to bring her here."

"Who's she?"

"I don't know," Tim replied dismissively. "Eric told me to bring her here. To Simon."

The henchman gave Lucy the appreciative eye elevator, up and down. Lucy didn't care.

"Fine," the man said. "Let's go."

He led them inside the department store, carrying a torch to light the way. It was dark and hot and stuffy. They crossed through the anchor store to its far side, where it connected with the interior of the mall. They passed by a jeweler, a computer store, and a clothing store popular with young women. The mall's access points were blocked off or guarded by armed men. Simon had taken control of the entire mall.

The henchman escorted them to a large sporting goods store and led them to the second floor. The place was awash in candlelight. Busy little bees. There were stacks of canned goods, piles of weapons, and pallets of bottled water scattered through the store. At the back of the store, near the camping and hunting supplies, three men sat around a table, illuminated by candlelight. It smelled of vanilla and pine. She didn't recognize them.

Their escort spoke first.

"Simon, this guy said Eric told him to bring the woman here."

"Who the fuck are you?" asked the man sitting in the middle. He was dressed casually in a pair of cargo shorts and a navy blue polo shirt. He was blonde, tanned, mid-thirties. Not what she expected. The man to his left was short, built like a hydrant. The third man was tall and lanky.

"Friend of Eric's," replied Tim.

"That right?"

"Yes."

"Where's Eric?"

"Said his girlfriend was getting suspicious."

"So?"

"He wanted to make sure he delivered the package to you like he agreed to."

Angela had confirmed Lucy's suspicions in their last conversation. Eric had cut a deal to trade Lucy and Norah to Simon for supplies and protection. That was why Eric had extended their visa. The mission to the distribution warehouse had been a ruse to get rid of Manny, divide and conquer them and leave Norah and Lucy unaware at Angela's. But when Lucy had insisted on joining the supply run, it had thrown a wrench into the plans. And if Eric had refused to let her tag along, it would have drawn suspicion. Even if he hadn't delivered Lucy, Eric would have been handsomely rewarded for bringing them Norah.

And now, this insane plan. It was the only way to get close to Norah again.

Simon got out of his chair, took a step toward Lucy, cupped her chin in between his thumb and forefinger. He smelled like body spray. Probably something with a ridiculous name like Arctic Tiger or Tropic Hellion.

"Well, well, well, what do we have here?" he said.

He took a step back and clapped his hands together.

"Whoo!" he cried out. "An embarrassment of riches today!"

He circled her like a shark.

"I know this is scary," he said, leaning in close to her ear. "But you're safer than you realize."

Lucy wanted to punch him in the throat. But she listened.

"It's been five days since the blackout," he said. "Five days, and the world has changed forever. You understand that, right?"

Lucy nodded.

"You wouldn't believe some of the things I've seen already," he said. "There's no food. People are already starving. Less than a week, and we've reverted to savagery. I know that's hard to believe. But it's true. People are dying every day. Every day. Innocent people like you are dying every day. But it doesn't have to be that way. I'm going to find you a new place to live. Someone who can provide for you."

He turned her face one way and then the other.

"You're a little older than I normally like," he said.

Her stomach turned.

"But you are beautiful. I don't think we'll have too much trouble with you."

He nodded dramatically.

"No trouble at all."

He gestured to the two men sitting at the table. They had not made a sound.

"Jeremy, take her downstairs, put her with the girl," he said.

Lucy's heart soared. Norah.

Jeremy took her by the elbow.

"I'll be on my way then," Tim said. "Eric said he would pay me later."

"No, no, no, no," he said rapidly. "I don't know what's going on here, but I'm going to hang on to you until I figure out what's going on with Eric."

"IIey, wait a minute," Tim said.

"Go find out what happened to Eric," he said to the other man, ignoring Tim's pleas. "He was a hard worker."

The man left on his mission. Simon grabbed Lucy and Tim by their ears.

"If I find out you were lying, I'm not going to be happy."

23

The mall had three holding cells located in a security office on the first floor, about a five-minute walk from Simon's nerve center in the sporting goods store. In less-apocalyptic days, mall security officers had detained shoplifters and people who'd had a bit too much to drink here until police could come collect them. She debated trying to escape en route to the cells, but it would be too risky until she confirmed that Norah was here. This would be her only chance to save the girl. Simon's henchmen guided them past the dark security office and to the small cellblock in the back. It was pitch black but for the tiny circle of flame kicked off by Jeremy's candle.

Tim went into the cell closest to the door, buttressing one of the security office walls; The cells were small, no more than six-by-six square; they were not designed for long-term use. The thug escorted Lucy to the third cell, passing the middle one and briefly illuminating it in a pool of shimmery orange. A small figure was lying on the cot in the corner.

It was Norah. Relief coursed through Lucy's veins. So far, the plan had worked. The commotion drew Norah's attention, and she sat up on her cot. After locking the cell doors, their jailer left them alone. As the room fell out of the candle's reach, a desolate darkness fell over the cells.

"Lucy?" she whispered.

"I'm here," Lucy said, extending her hand through the bars. "Take my hand."

Norah reached out; their fingers laced together in the void of space and time. Norah began to cry.

"Shhh," Lucy said. "I'm here."

The girl cried for a little while; then the tears subsided, and she was calm again.

"You okay?" Lucy asked.

"Yeah," she replied, her voice cracking a bit.

"Good. We're gonna be okay."

"Okay."

"Tim?"

"Present," he said with a hint of jocularity. Lucy smiled.

"You good?" she whispered.

"Fine."

"Sorry you got caught up in this," she said. "I should've seen that coming."

"Don't sweat it. I knew there was a risk."

"Couldn't help yourself, huh?"

"What can I say?" he replied. "I'm drawn to trouble."

"How are things at the school?"

"Good," he said. "We're down to about twenty kids. Parents keep showing up. Six other teachers are still there."

He fell silent. She felt badly for him. He would be kicking himself for leaving his colleagues in the lurch. But she couldn't fault him for it. The kids were safe. They had plenty of adult supervision. And he was looking after someone he'd cared about. Whether he should have cared about her was a different matter.

"What now?" he asked.

"Working on it," she said.

She explored the limits of the cell, checking the bars and the wall, looking for a weakness she could exploit. Damp walls and cold bars. Not much. She felt her way through the darkness toward the cot and lay down to collect her thoughts. The cells were silent but for the soft breathing of her companions. The darkness was rich and deep and eternal. Lucy had never encountered such darkness. It was a presence, an almost living, breathing entity. As she lay on her back, it felt like she was floating. Panic fluttered through her. Simon would soon learn that Eric was dead. She was running out of time.

"Lucy."

"What's wrong?"

"I'm scared."

"I know."

A few seconds of silence, each second stretching interminably, an eternity unto itself. She felt like she was the only living thing in the universe.

"You came for me," said Norah.

"You didn't think I was gonna leave you here by yourself, did you?"

A half laugh, half sob.

"Just stay calm, and I'm gonna get us out of here."

But that was easier said than done.

Lucy examined every square inch of the cell a second time, every bar, every bit of the tile floor, every centimeter of the concrete wall. But there was nothing in the cell but a cot, a thin sheet, and a pillow.

She lay back down. She would have to think of another way.

"Lucy?"

"Yeah?"

"Can you tell me a story?" asked Norah.

"Sure."

And so Lucy told Norah the story that she had told Emma dozens of times, the story she had told Emma on her last night on earth, the one she told her just a few minutes before she died. The story was about a brave little girl in a faraway land named Aurora, who had saved her village from a powerful wizard. As Lucy told it to Norah, in the dark, in the black, she was back with Emma in her bedroom, the last treatment given, the last hope exhausted. There was morphine Emma could self-administer, and the nurses promised Lucy that she was not in any pain. The horror of a child self-administering morphine haunted Lucy even now five years after her death. Emma slept most of the time, twenty hours a day. The rest of the time, she was in a peaceful, semiconscious haze. Lucy sat with her, held her hand, kissed her cheek.

In the story, which Lucy had first heard from her own mother many years earlier, the little girl had traveled deep into the woods to find the wizard who had stolen all the babies from the village. In the end, the little girl had tricked the wizard into transferring his magic to her, which she then used to banish him from their world.

"And they lived happily ever after," she said.

"That was a good story."

Tears fell from Lucy's eyes, splashing her arms.

Emma had passed away a few minutes after Lucy had finished telling the story. It was just the two of them in the room; the nurse had gone to use the restroom, but she had told Lucy that it wouldn't be long. Lucy had known the nurse, a veteran named Christine Brown; Lucy suspected that the she had timed the bathroom break to give mother and daughter time alone together at the end, for which Lucy was forever grateful. Nurses knew when the end was at hand. When it was just the two of them, it didn't seem like Emma was dying. It just seemed like Emma was taking a nap.

"What was your favorite part?"

"When Aurora tricked the wizard."

Lucy laugh-cried at that. That had been Emma's favorite part as well.

"Yeah, that's my favorite too."

When Aurora had tricked the wizard.

As they sat there in the dark, an idea came to her. It was extremely risky and was as likely to end in her death as not. But it was not a bad plan. Not too bad at all.

"Hey, Norah?"

"Yeah?"

"You wanna get out of here?"

"Definitely."

"Can you do exactly what I tell you?"

"Yes, ma'am."

"Tim, can you hear me?"

"Roger that."

She told Norah and Tim her plan.

Lucy rattled the cell door with both of her hands.

"Hey!" she called out. "Hey, we need help in here!"

Tim mimicked Lucy's calls for help, rattling his own cell door. Combined with their pleas for help, they made an ear-piercing racket. It sounded desperate. Terribly desperate, which was precisely the point. It took a while, at least ten minutes of raising holy hell, but eventually, it drew a response.

A figure appeared in the doorway, carrying a candle. It was Jeremy, the man who'd escorted them here.

"Hey, knock that shit off!" he barked. "Or I'll give you something to scream about."

"Something's wrong with the girl."

"What are you talking about?"

"She's sick."

"How do you know?"

"I'm a nurse," replied Lucy. "I know."

"What's wrong with her?"

"She's diabetic. I'm guessing her blood sugar is low. Her symptoms are consistent with hypoglycemia."

"Hypo-what?"

"Dammit, her blood sugar is low," she repeated, this time much more loudly. "Did I stutter? She needs sugar now."

"A candy bar?"

"Pure sugar will work the fastest," she said.

That wasn't entirely true, but this idiot didn't know that.

"I'm gonna get Simon," he said.

"Fine," Lucy said. "You can explain to him why she's dead."

"Dead?"

"This is a goddamn emergency," Lucy snapped. "We don't have time for you to go up the chain of command. Please do not let this girl die."

He stepped toward Norah's cell and tilted the candle,

spilling light toward her cot. Norah was curled up in a fetal position.

"Maybe she's just asleep."

"Trust me, she is not just asleep."

"Maybe she's just tired."

"Touch her forehead," Lucy said.

"I'm not supposed to open the cell."

"Then just trust me. She needs sugar now."

"Fine," he said, exhaling nervously. "How much sugar?"

"Bring a cup's worth," she said. "And hurry."

He left quickly, plunging the cell block back into darkness. Lucy waited for a minute before speaking.

"Great job, kid," she whispered.

"Did I do good?"

"Perfect," she said. "Get up and run in place again for a minute. As hard as you can."

Norah got up and repeated the ruse, sprinting in place as hard as she could for thirty seconds. Lucy kept an eye out for the telltale sign of the return of their captors, the orange-red glow of candlelight. Norah's breathing grew rapid and shallow as she exerted herself.

Then the slightest hint of light.

"Okay, now!" she hissed.

The cot creaked as Norah lay back down.

The glow intensified as the visitor drew closer to the cells. The man appeared in the doorway, his hands occupied with a candle and a paper cup. But it wasn't the same man this time.

It was Simon.

"What's the problem here?"

Lucy sighed.

"Do you want to discuss it or do you want to save her?"

His face twisted into a grimace as he considered the predicament. Finally, he removed a key hanging from his belt and unlocked the cell door.

"See for yourself," Lucy said. "She's probably got a fever. Check her forehead."

He knelt down next to Norah and lay a hand on her forehead.

"She's burning up."

"Check her pulse."

"How?"

"Gently press your first two fingers to the underside of her wrist."

He did so.

"Start counting beats," she said. "I'll tell you when to stop."

"It's really fast."

"Just count."

She counted off fifteen seconds.

"How many?"

"Fifty or so?"

"That's two hundred beats per minute."

"Is that bad?"

"Yes, it's extremely bad," Lucy said firmly. "For a kid that age, her heart rate should be around ninety. Now do you believe me?"

"Do I just give it to her?"

"No," she said. "You need to let me do it."

"What?"

"It has to be titrated properly," she said. "Do you know how to do that?"

He shook his head.

"I don't know what that means."

"Then let me out and I'll take care of it."

Simon groaned loudly.

"Look, I just want to make sure she's okay," Lucy said reassuringly. "If I run, she dies."

He groaned a second time.

"Believe me, I would love to get out of here," she said. "That's no secret, right?"

"I guess."

"But I'm not going to let her die," she said. "I'm a nurse. I work with kids. I, uh…"

Lucy debated using the memory of her late daughter against this man.

"We're running out of time."

"Just tell me how to do it," Simon said.

"There's no time," Lucy said. "You got kids?"

"Yeah. A son."

"Then you know what it's like to be a parent," she said. "I had a daughter once. She died of cancer. I won't let this girl die to save myself. You have my word."

Lucy hated that Simon now knew about Emma, but if it worked, then it would have been worth it. Emma would have been okay with it. After an interminable moment, Simon sighed, relenting to Lucy's pressure. He unlocked Lucy's cell door; then he handed the cup to Lucy and guided her to Norah's cell. He drew his weapon and aimed it at Lucy's head as she knelt to the prone girl.

"No funny business," he said. "I mean it."

"Just help me here," she said. "We need to place about a teaspoon of sugar between her lip and the back of her gums every two minutes. Can you hold the candle close to her face for me?"

"What do you need me for? Just put it in her mouth!"

"No. It has to be like a slow drip. If her blood sugar rises too quickly, it could stop her heart. And it has to be in the right spot, right behind her back molars."

This was a complete load of bullshit, but she said it with authority, and no one ever questioned a health care professional when she said something with authority. That was the key to everything. Fake it until you make it. The truism had applied in the old world, and it definitely applied in their current nightmare.

"Fine, Jesus, just hurry."

"Okay, let's slide her over toward the edge of the bed."

As they worked, she kept an eye on his handling of the weapon. He'd removed his finger from the trigger guard as he gently grabbed her shoulders while Lucy took her by the ankles.

"Okay," she said. "I need you to tilt her head up toward me and hold her mouth open."

Lucy sprinkled about a teaspoon of the sugar into her

cupped fingers; she didn't care if her measurement was exact. As they had discussed, Norah resisted when Simon tried to work her mouth open.

"She won't open her mouth."

"Shit, she might be having a seizure."

"Oh shit," said Simon.

"You need to use both hands to get her jaw open," Lucy ordered. "Give me the candle."

Without giving it a second thought, he set the gun down on the cot and handed the candle to Lucy. Then he set to work working Norah's mouth open.

"Be firm, but not too firm," she said.

He nodded. He was sweating heavily, his face intent on his work. He had bought the ruse hook, line, and sinker. Now, for the payoff.

"It's working!" he said.

Norah's mouth was slowly opening. Lucy rubbed the sugar against Norah's gums, keeping an eye fixed on Simon. He was completely distracted. She would only get one shot.

She took it.

She threw the cup of sugar in his eyes. At such close range, the effect was massive. Millions of grains of sugar flew into his eyes, immediately but temporarily blinding him. It was a direct hit; most of the sugar flew square into his eyeballs. Then she held the candle to his face, immediately igniting the oxygen in the interstitials of the cloud of sugar. The candle's tiny corona of flame bloomed rapidly; he screamed in agony, falling over backwards.

"You bitch!" he screamed as he understood the ruse, pawing at his damaged eyes.

He kicked out at her, but he was much too focused on the devastating injury Lucy had unleashed. He continued rolling around on the ground, screaming. She had to act quickly; his screams would quickly draw attention from the others. She turned to grab the gun from the cot. In the meantime, Simon got his hands on her neck; he slid them around her throat and began to squeeze; he was still howling in pain, but he managed to secure a firm hold on Lucy's windpipe. Instinctively, she bucked against him, her body desperate to draw in oxygen and unable to do so.

She drove her legs into his chest, which loosened his grip on her throat. He swung wildly, the back of his hand connecting against her skull and knocking her against the wall. He was still moaning, still hobbled by her chemical attack. He had crumpled to the ground, his hands clawing at his eyes. For the time being, his interest in self-preservation outweighed his desire to end Lucy's life. The cellblock keys were hanging from his waist. She delivered a kick to his head, which totally immobilized him. She grabbed the keys and set to work freeing Tim from his cell.

"Let's go," she said.

When both Tim and Norah were clear of their cells, she touched the candle to both cots, igniting them. She didn't know how far the blaze would spread, but any diversion would be welcome as they made their escape. She took care to keep her candle lit.

The smoke thickened quickly as they took their leave of the cellblock.

.

24

They edged their way toward the door, the heat from the rapidly spreading blaze warming their backs. Already, thick smoke was pouring out behind them, trickling through the gaps in the walls. Taking Norah's hand, Lucy followed the left corridor as the fire raced along with them. They were in the traditional section of the mall, the one she remembered from her youth. As they moved through the mall, she tipped over the torches that Simon's people had set up at short intervals, triggering additional fires in their wake.

In the dark, shouts and yells burst forth as it dawned on the lords of the mall that something was wrong. People were running in every direction, but no one paid them any mind. It was too dark to identify them as the captives.

At the end of the concourse, they reached a silent escalator. They took the steps two at a time, even Norah, her long legs carrying her as quickly as the adults. Halfway up the escalator, a loud explosion rocked the mall.

Fires were now burning on both levels. The flames looked like orange-red monsters consuming everything in the grasp of their fiery fingers. Lucy paused at the top of the escalator, taking stock of their location. Ironically, she could now see quite well; the flames were providing plenty of illumination.

Their problem was simple. They were trapped in the mall's interior section, much of which was now burning. They would have to find a point of egress, but it was unclear which access points remained clear of flames. And once they committed to one point of attack, she wasn't sure they'd get a chance to double back. By then, the interior of the mall might be fully engulfed.

Instead, the roaring blaze cracked and crackled and hissed and whispered in the great silence. It suddenly struck Lucy that no one would be coming to fight the fire; there would be no howl of sirens, no shouts of firemen, no hiss of water hoses and fire retardant called on to fight this terrible blaze.

The fire was moving. It was time to decide.

There was a skywalk halfway down the concourse, flying over the road below and connecting to the northern half of the mall. She led the group down the left concourse, but a chunk of burning ceiling came tumbling down, partially blocking the way. They ducked into a darkened gourmet kitchen store and huddled behind a display of cast-iron pans. A sea of fire had washed across the lower level.

The look on Norah's face was one of fright. Tim didn't look much better.

They had to get out of here. She did not come all this way, go through all they'd gone through these last five days to die in this godforsaken altar to consumerism. They needed to get to the skywalk. She checked the concourse again. There appeared to be a narrow gap in between the burning chunk and the wall. If they threaded it just so, they might have a chance.

"Follow me."

They retraced their steps down the concourse, edging close to the wall as they approached the burning monolith.

"On my shoulders," she ordered Norah, dropping down to her knees.

The girl hitched herself onto Lucy's back. Lucy stood up, Norah's arms and legs wrapped around her like a baby cub on her mother's back. Once Norah was secure, she began the trek as quickly as she could manage, threading the needle to safety. The warmth nibbled at her skin; the speed at which the fire had grown was almost unfathomable. Norah screamed as the flames licked at them. The smell of burning hair filled Lucy's nose. Sweat flowed into her eyes like rivers, making it even more difficult to see. All three of them were coughing heavily. Her back and legs ached, but she would not stop. Tim was close behind, keeping a hand at her back to stabilize her.

Then they were through. She eased Norah to the ground and took a huge breath, but the thickening smoke triggered a heavy coughing fit. They were not out of the woods yet. Another fire had sprung up on the far side of the skywalk, cutting off that route of escape.

"Shit," she muttered.

"What now?" Tim asked.

She pointed at the bridge.

"We need to rappel down the side."

"With what?"

"We'll jerry-rig something together."

She studied the immediate vicinity. They were near a small store selling lotions, bath soaps, candles, and other sundry items designed to make your home smell like a potpourri bomb had exploded. Next door to that was a woman's clothing store. She swept into the store like she was storming a beachhead, grabbing pants and tops and scarves, as many as she could gather into her arms. She ran back to the skywalk, the long sleeves and pant legs from her scavenging mission streaming behind her like party streamers.

"Tie these together," she said, handing the armful of clothing to Tim. "Start making a rope. As many knots as you can. Keep the knots close together. That will keep it strong."

She made another pass through the store, finding a collection of belts on a rack near the back. These would help strengthen the makeshift escape rope like rebar; it would have to do, as the smoke was getting too thick to risk another sortie. Back at the skywalk, Tim and Norah had made good progress, tying together sleeves and pant legs, triple-knotting short segments. Another explosion rocked the mall, this one large enough to shake the building and take Lucy's breath away. Norah began to cry.

"Stay calm, honey," Lucy said. "We'll be out of here before you know it."

She nodded.

"Let's test it."

She and Tim each took an end of the rope, which had grown to about twenty feet long, the knots spaced at one-foot increments.

"You stand there," she said to Tim, pointing to a spot near the edge of the bridge.

"Norah, you and I are gonna pull as hard as we can on this end," she said. Then she signaled to Tim, who'd wrapped the end of the rope around his forearm.

Together, she and Norah pulled on it as hard as they could. She wrapped an arm around the railing of the skywalk to add some additional leverage and strain on their rope. It held. It wasn't perfect, but this was as good a field test as they would get. Gravity would add additional strain on the rope. How much remained to be seen; they'd just have to hope the rope was strong enough.

Lucy secured the end of the rope to the railing. She triple-looped the end of the rope around the railing, leaving enough slack to tie multiple knots. Then she tied off the slack with the gnarliest knot she'd learned in basic training.

"Okay, Norah, you first."

She shook her head violently.

"I'm scared," she said.

She knelt down and took Norah by her narrow shoulders.

"Listen to me," she said. "I know you're scared. It's okay to be scared. But you can be brave and scared at the same time. Did you know that?"

She shook her head.

"Want to know a secret?" Lucy asked.

"Yes."

"I'm scared too."

"You are?"

"Of course," said Lucy. "What we're about to do is scary. I'm not gonna tell you it's not. But we can be brave at the same time. Brave means being scared to do something important and then doing it anyway. Does that make sense?"

Norah nodded her head.

"Okay," said the girl.

"Ready?"

She nodded her head again.

Lucy and Tim looped the end of the rope around Norah's waist three times, and then twice between her legs, forming a makeshift harness. Lucy checked and double checked the knots, looking for any weaknesses they'd missed.

"Just untie it when you get to the bottom, and we'll pull it back up for us."

Norah threw her arms around Lucy and hugged her tightly; Lucy hugged her back.

"It's gonna be okay."

Columns of fire were approaching both ends of the skyway now, leaving no other route of escape. So this was it. They would either escape or they would die. She closed her eyes; it was time to make her peace with it. She was with Emma now, feeling as close to her as she ever had. Emma had been brave. She had done all the things that needed to be done and never once betrayed a sliver of fear. There was even a tiny part of her that thought maybe it wouldn't be the worst thing in the world, dying here, if there was a chance to be reunited with Emma. Just lay down and let the smoke take her.

"Lucy!"

Norah's sweet voice snapped her back to reality. She couldn't give up now; she had to save this girl, and then she had to keep her safe in this bizarre new world. She checked the harness a second time; they had made it as secure they could. The smoke was thickening, filling the air with its poisonous gases.

"Tim, lift her over the railing," she said.

Her voice was small and tight.

They were silent as they moved into this final critical phase. Lucy held the rope even though it was securely tied to the railing. Tim eased her over the side; Norah was breathing rapidly, but her face was clear and severe. She seemed to grasp that this was the only chance they had left.

"Okay, let her go."

Tim hesitated; Lucy understood his reluctance. If they didn't execute this part perfectly, the girl would tumble two stories to her death. She placed a gentle hand on his back.

"It'll hold."

She tightened her grip on the rope as Tim slowly released his grip on Norah. The harness held, and she swayed gently in the breeze.

"Give her some rope now," Tim said.

Lucy eased her downward, hand over hand, one at a time. The rope dug into her hands, but the tether held.

"Halfway down now," called out Tim.

She continued releasing the slack, closing her eyes, her forearms burning, her body roasting in the wake of the approaching flames. She half-expected the rope to snap, her ears filling with the girl's screams as she plunged to her death.

"Almost there," Tim called out. "Almost. Almost."

Then Lucy felt a great relief in her arms as the resistance suddenly disappeared. A storm of panic followed, Lucy thinking the rope had finally broken.

"She's down," he called out.

Lucy peered down over the railing. Norah was firmly on the ground and working to undo the knots of the harness.

"Great job, honey!" she called out.

She patted Tim on the shoulder.

"Your turn."

"No."

"Look, I got you in this mess," she said. "The least I can do is make sure you get out of it. Besides, I'm lighter than you. It'll be easier for me to come down with the rope tied to the railing. Don't bother arguing."

"You're sure?"

"Now."

Tim held the railing and then pivoted his body over onto the sliver of ledge. He carefully took hold of the rope and then let go. Like Norah, he swung in the breeze before beginning his rappel. Lucy held her segment tightly, eyeing the knot tied to the railing. It was holding, but the strain on it was obvious, the rope stretching taut. If she hadn't been there to absorb the weight, it wasn't at all clear it would hold.

Then he was down. Tears filled her eyes as she watched Tim and Norah embrace. They were so close now. It was her turn.

"Coming down!" she called down.

So close.

She climbed over the railing and took hold of the rope. She wrapped her legs around the rope and began lowering herself down. The makeshift rope strained against the railing, but it was holding. Her stomach was in her throat as she danced on this razor's edge between life and death. She kept edging her way down the rope, conscious that she didn't need to make it to the ground to ensure she survived.

"Lucy!"

She glanced down. Tim was furiously waving his arms, pointing skyward. She looked up and saw someone at the railing. Simon. He had managed to escape the firestorm in the security office. He started sawing at the rope with a knife. She increased her pace. Panic shot through her. She was still about a full story off the ground.

"Hurry up, Lucy!" screamed Norah.

She was ten feet off the ground when the rope snapped.

The ground rushed up at her and she braced herself for the impact.

Her body lit up with pain as she hit the ground. There had been no time to curl up into a roll, which might have helped dissipate some of her kinetic energy. No such luck. She felt every last bit of it. But that was a good sign too, in that she had felt it. She lay on the ground in a heap.

They had made it.

Tim rushed to her side and helped her to her feet. Standard protocols for a neck or back injury didn't apply right now, given the threat from above. Her body was still functioning, and that would be enough for now. They rushed out of Simon's line of sight, curling around a corner. They were in the middle of the street, surrounded by dead vehicles. No one paid them any mind as the Ballston Mall continued to burn behind them.

Tim ushered her and Norah to safety behind a wall, out of view of the top of the skywalk. Norah threw her skinny little arms around Lucy's waist, causing her to wince, but it felt wonderful all the same. She had kept Norah safe. She had taken the worst of what this world offered them so far, and she had prevailed.

"We made it," Tim said to no one in particular. "We made it."

His face was wild with emotion, his smile huge, his eyes wide.

"I thought we were all dead," he said, his words coming at a rapid clip. "When he said he was gonna lock me up, I thought that was it. There was no way out. No one coming to help us."

"What do we do now?" he asked.

"We go home."

25

F
ifteen days.

It took them fifteen days, but they made it.

Near dusk on their final day on the road, they crested a hill. Lucy paused. Her small farm lay below them in a shallow valley. They were in Goochland County, a geographically large but lightly populated rural county just west of the Richmond metropolitan area. Lucy had lived here for four years; she and Jack had inherited the place from her late parents but only moved out here after Emma had passed away. They had four acres, much of the land arable. She and her brother saw to the land themselves; he worked it full-time and lived in the guesthouse.

The sun was setting; it had been a beautiful day for travel, made all the more so by the knowledge that they would be home by dinnertime. The sun sparkled across her rich farmland; the summer crops were starting to come to a head. Everything was green and verdant; rain had been plentiful in her absence. At least Mother Nature hadn't needed to rely on man these last few weeks. She had taken care of herself as society had torn itself apart at the seams. She always could. They were still a mile off, but in the distance, she spotted a solitary figure working the land.

Her brother. The man she trusted most of all in the world. The man she trusted least of all in the world. She loved him dearly, as younger sisters often loved their older brothers, but sometimes, she hated him as well.

"There it is," she whispered to Norah.

After escaping the mall, they had spent the night in a convenience store a couple of miles away. Unfortunately, it had been stripped clean and there were no supplies to be had. Norah slept deeply while Lucy and Tim traded watch. No one approached the store, and the night passed in relative peace. Constant gunfire served as a constant reminder of the dangers that awaited them at every turn. The next morning dawned cool and cloudy. The power was still out. Still no idea what lay ahead. But they were safe.

"Why don't you come to Richmond with me?" she asked Tim.

"You serious?"

"Very," she said. "Look, I'm not asking you to marry me or anything. But you're a good man. And it's gonna be pretty rough in the cities while the power is out. Even in that school of yours."

She didn't know why she was pressing him so hard to join her. She wasn't attracted to him, but she did like him quite a bit. He was a good man who deserved better than having to fend for himself in the city. Good people were going to have a rough go of it for a while. Good people didn't think about themselves first, and they certainly did not think about taking advantage of others.

"I've got a little farm just west of the city. Some chickens and sheep. It'll keep us fed for a while. You're gonna have the same issues if you make it back to your house, you know. And as soon as the power cuts back on, I'm kicking you out on the street," she added playfully.

"I appreciate the offer, but I can't abandon the school," he said. "I've gotta make sure those kids are safe."

Lucy understood. In fact, she would have been surprised if he'd taken her up on the offer.

"I just can't believe the power is still out," he said. "I didn't think it would last this long. I really didn't."

She felt the same way. Accepting their new reality was hard. Grief coursed through her, not dissimilar to the grief she had felt after Emma had passed. But not entirely the same. This was a mourning of not just what had already happened, like Manny's death, but also of things yet to pass. When you got to the middle part of your life, you were pretty set in your ways, pretty set in accepting your environment as your reality. When something came along to tear that asunder, it could be quite the shock. Being able to adapt to this new reality would be a critical skill for everyone. Her, Tim, Norah, Jack, everyone.

"No one wants to believe the worst will happen," replied Lucy.

"Yeah. What happens if it doesn't come back?"

She considered his question.

"The first to figure that out wins," she replied ominously.

They stood silently; there was nothing more to be said.

"You take care of yourselves," he said.

They hugged. He knelt down and gave Norah a hug as well.

"You take care of Lucy here, okay?"

Norah nodded, a big smile on her face.

"If things don't get better soon, and you need to get out of the city, you come to my farm, okay? I mean that."

"Okay."

She wrote down directions to the farm on the back of a flyer on the store counter. He tucked it in his pocket. Then he was gone. They watched him disappear into the morning gloom.

She and Norah made it ten miles the first day, sliding westward until they picked up Route 1, which ran the spine of the eastern seaboard from Maine to Florida. They stayed close to or in the woods paralleling the highway much of the way. There wasn't much to eat, but fortunately, it had rained quite a bit during their two-week trek southward. They searched every abandoned vehicle they encountered; they found something worth salvaging in one out of every ten cars or so. Half-eaten bags of chips. Bags of raisins. Just enough fuel to keep them moving.

It was a hell of a journey, far different from the one they'd undertaken from Union Station to Angela's house. Out here in the boonies, the effect of the Pulse was far less pronounced. No less catastrophic, of course, what with the loss of electricity and motorized transport, but it wasn't hitting home quite as hard.

They passed grain silos and farms and diners and small ranch homes with plastic toys strewn about the yard. They got suspicious looks, and they got waves. Every once in a while, they fell into a chat with someone who wanted the same thing they did: information.

Down from D.C.

No, it's the same there.

Worse actually.

Took us days to get out of the city.

About a week into their remarkable journey south, a generous farmer took them in for the night and offered them a home-cooked meal. They spent the night in the barn, but it was a warm and pleasant night; they slept soundly in the hay that smelled richly of earth and dirt and things that grew in the ground.

If there was one takeaway from this trip, it was that

the cities were no place to be right now. She didn't know what that would mean for people who lived in the cities, who would soon run out of vital supplies if they hadn't already. Conflict would explode once demand for resources outstripped the supply.

She was glad to be home. She was glad she could see her farm. She glanced over at Norah; the kid was dead on her feet. The hundred-mile march south had taken its toll on her lithe body. Her small frame had thinned out even more. Her first priority would be tending to the girl's health.

But first, they had to finish the journey.

They were on a narrow country road, Route 516, which gently wound its way through a neighboring farm's tobacco fields and passed the entrance to her farm on the west. The sun was high and broiling the land below. But the sun felt good on her shoulders, her dirty shoulders, her exhausted body.

They were about a quarter-mile away when Jack spotted them. He was working the fields with an old-fashioned hoe as this new pre-technological period would have demanded.

Jack.

She wondered how he'd handled the last two weeks. Had he assumed that she was dead? Or had he had faith in her abilities to take care of herself? He was older than she was, a lifelong bachelor, no kids. He had taught her self-reliance. He would've been disappointed in her if she hadn't been able to handle herself.

He was waiting for them on the wraparound porch at the front of the house. He was sitting in the old rocking chair, beaten to gray by the elements and by time itself, smoking a cigarette. A shotgun was propped up against the siding. Despite the heat, Jack wore jeans and a flannel shirt. His light brown hair was speckled with gray, and a pair of rimless glasses made him look more like a lawyer or professor than a farmer and small-time con man. He crushed the cigarette out in the heavy, amber-colored ash tray that had existed since the dawn of time and blew out a thin stream of smoke.

"You look like shit," he said, but not in a mean way.

"I feel like it," she replied.

He got out of the chair and embraced her tightly. She was a bit taken aback by the display of affection. When he pulled back from her, there were tears in his eyes.

"I had kind of given up hope, to be honest," he said. "I figured even if you had to walk back from Philly, you would have been back by now."

"We got held up."

"Sounds like quite a story."

"It is."

As best as she could tell, nearly a month had passed since that terrible day in Washington, D.C., the day shadows had covered the world in darkness. It felt like a lifetime.

"This is Norah," she said, pulling the girl close to her. "We're gonna look after her for a while."

He nodded at the girl. Her brother didn't have any

kids (that she knew of), but he had an easy way with
children.

NIGHT HAD FALLEN.

Unable to sleep, Lucy wandered the small house,
awed by the ordinary, the peace, the quiet of home. Her
couch, the pictures she hung on the walls, the books on
the bookshelves she had read but could not bear to part
with. Lanterns burned in every room, simultaneously
ominous and warm. She heard the heavy thwack of Jack's
lighter on the porch, and so she joined him for a drink.

A kerosene lantern burned on the table in between
them as they shared a bourbon, washing the porch in
warm orange light. Norah had been asleep for hours,
crashing as soon as she ate dinner. Jack had cooked up
fresh eggs and potatoes over a fire; Norah had polished
off four eggs herself.

Overhead, in a clear sky, the stars shone brightly, a
million billion of them reflecting their dead light toward
them.

"How've things been here?" she asked.

"About the same," he replied. "Most of the folks out
here are pretty well-stocked for the summer. We've had
good rains, so the crops are really solid. Not too bad.
Might be a different story come winter if things don't
come back."

She sipped the bourbon, enjoying the oak flavor as it swirled in her mouth. She had told him about the train crash, their journey to Arlington, their desperate battle to escape Simon. It seemed so small, their struggle, so insignificant against a backdrop of such catastrophe.

"You really didn't get any news about what happened?" she asked.

"Not a thing."

"Damn."

Jack had surmised, incorrectly, as it turned out, that she would have gleaned some intelligence about the nature of the cataclysm that had upended their lives. He was surprised that there wasn't at least some semblance of order in the urban areas she'd been in.

"So we're on our own."

"Seems that way," she replied.

This wouldn't faze him one way or the other. Jack Goodwin was accountable to no one but himself. Interested in no one but himself. Second, a distant second, was family. He had loved Emma fiercely, but after she had died, he had turned inward even more.

That's the way she would have to be now. For Norah. For herself.

A great deal of work lay ahead of them.

Many challenges.

Many dangers.

She would be ready.

The Story Continues in NIGHTFALL
Download NIGHTFALL Now

Sign up for my mailing list at my website and get two exclusive pieces of content.

DOWNLOAD NIGHTFALL NOW!

THE SECOND BOOK IN THE
AMERICAN MIDNIGHT SERIES

NIGHTFALL

AFTERWORD

I began writing SHADOWS in the late summer of 2019, and I finished the first draft in the early morning hours of December 31, 2019. That same day, China notified the World Health Organization about several unusual cases of pneumonia in Wuhan. Little did we know that our lives were about to change forever.

I continued working on the manuscript as the outbreak worsened and spread worldwide. By March, it was clear that we were in for a very rough ride in the United States, and it became increasingly difficult to focus on fiction. In particular, it became difficult to work on this *kind* of fiction, and part of me considered abandoning this book and the planned series altogether. I mean, who wants to read about the end of the world while a pandemic is raging outside our window?

But I liked the book, and I'm still excited about the rest of the series. And it's been therapeutic living with characters who are dealing with difficult challenges beyond their control just as we are. If I begin to waver in my resolve, I can look to Lucy, Norah, and Tim for strength.

I also struggled with whether to incorporate the coronavirus pandemic into this story. Unless you're one of the weird ones (like me) who reads Afterwords first, you'll know that SHADOWS is set in a world where the coronavirus pandemic did happen. It seemed too big an event to gloss over given the towering impact it's had on all of our lives.

As I write this Afterword, we've been on lockdown for more than a month, and we have more than a month to go in my home state before we begin the first phase of reopening. It's been difficult and frightening at times, and there is no way to know how it will all turn out. Due to the unique nature of books, I have no idea when you're reading this. With any luck, as you read these words, the pandemic is behind us and we are in a safer and better world.

But even if the pandemic is still ongoing as you read this, I am confident that we will get through it together.

We will get through it with medicine and science, with music and food, with fresh air and exercise, and most importantly, with connection and love.

And the occasional end of the world story.

David Kazzie
April 2020

ACKNOWLEDGMENTS

To my Advance Reader Team, thank you for your feedback, support and encouragement as I bring this new series to life.

To Dave Buckley, thank you for standing on the front lines of my first drafts.

To Ali Funk, thank you for your careful and meticulous work proofreading the final draft.

All errors are mine alone.

ABOUT THE AUTHOR

David's first novel, *The Jackpot*, was a No.1 bestselling legal thriller. He is also the author of *The Immune*, *The Living*, *Anomaly,* and *The Nothing Men*.

His short comedy films about law and publishing have amassed more than 2.5 million hits on YouTube and were featured on CNN, in *The Washington Post*, *The Huffington Post*, and *The Wall Street Journal*.

Visit him at his website or follow him on Facebook (David Kazzie, Author) and Twitter (@davidkazzie).

Made in the USA
Coppell, TX
22 July 2023

19490292R00185